MORE THAN
PUPPY LOVE

HIGH SCHOOL REUNION & FRIENDS TO
LOVERS ROMANTIC SHORT STORY

REGINA MORRIS

MORE THAN PUPPY LOVE

Regina Morris
Smashwords Edition
Join Regina Morris' mailing list for games, freebies, and
fun at
http://newsletter.reginamorris.com
Please visit author Regina Morris on her website
http://www.reginamorris.com
Regina Morris enjoys connecting with fans on social
media. Please find her at:
Facebook: http://www.facebook.com/ReginaAnnMorris
(@ReginaMorris)
Twitter: http://www.twitter.com/ReginaMorris
(@ReginaMorris)
Pinterest: http://www.pinterest.com/ReginaAnnMorris

Ex-wallflower, now a veterinarian, Kacie Preston is eager
to go to her ten-year high school reunion where she can
meet up with the boy she crushed on for years. But then

his dog, her patient, shows up at the event mistreated. How well does Kacie know her old heart throb?

Silkhaven Publishing, LLC

ISBN: 978-1-948997-01-0 (mobi)

ISBN: 978-1-948997-02-7 (epub)

ISBN: 978-1-948997-03-4 (paperback)

Library of Congress Control Number: 2018904993

Copyright (c) 2015, Regina Morris

(V3) – November 18, 2022

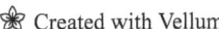 Created with Vellum

CONTENTS

Chapter 1	1
Chapter 2	8
Chapter 3	12
Chapter 4	16
Chapter 5	22
Chapter 6	29
Chapter 7	40
Chapter 8	48
Chapter 9	56
Chapter 10	61
Chapter 11	68
Chapter 12	75
Chapter 13	79
Chapter 14	84
Chapter 15	86
Chapter 16	93
Epilogue	97
About the Author	101
Acknowledgments	103
Other Books by Regina Morris	105
Other Books by Regina Morris	107

K acie was aging, and her eggs were drying up.

It had been two days since her fiancé had called her, and the message from his assistant made her cringe. She clenched her cell phone tightly, making her knuckles turn white, and glared at the call log. Braiden didn't even have the decency to call her himself. She interacted more with his damn personal assistant than with the man she intended to marry in May.

Well, May of next year. They had postponed the wedding twice already.

"Why the long face?" Derrick's gaze darted from his boss to exam room #2. He focused on the long, sterile hallway of the vet clinic, his eyes filling with concern. "Will that cute puppy survive?"

A punch to her gut wounded her pride. She needed to work, not engage in a pity party. That hurt, three–month–old puppy was in her capable hands. She smoothed the wrinkles from her white hospital coat and focused on her job. "Jasper is fine. He needed stitches, and he'll wear a cone for six weeks, but he'll recover fully."

An expression of relief crossed Derrick's face. "I doubt that little fluff–ball will pick a fight with a raccoon again."

"Hopefully not for a long time." She pointed to a crate where a Sheltie puppy lay sleeping, his tiny head poking out of the smallest cone the vet clinic had. "I stitched up his ears and throat. His eyes took a beating, but they're all right. He's getting some IV fluids now and will spend the night here."

"I'm on call this weekend. I'll make sure he's comfortable." Derrick turned his focus to Kacie and frowned. "If Jasper's fine, why do you look like you have bad news to tell somebody?"

Kacie glanced at her cell phone. "It's nothing." She placed the device in the front pocket of her white coat and then let out a sigh, slow and sad.

"I'm your best friend. You know you're going to tell me anyway." Derrick grabbed a thermometer from behind the counter. "Before I check the vitals on the cat in room #1, do you want to tell me what's got you down?"

A pang of self–doubt crept over her. Another patient had come to her vet clinic, and she didn't even know. How many patients did that make today? Four? Keeping the place open would prove difficult with so few. She wanted to make a difference for the animals of this community, but she was falling short. "I'll examine the cat."

"Kitty can wait. He only needs his annual shots, and I haven't done his vitals yet." Derrick cocked his eyebrow and tilted his head. In an all-knowing voice, he asked, "What did Braiden do this time?"

She kept nothing from Derrick. Being one of the few employees she could afford, he always seemed underfoot. He was also her best friend. Of course, she was an open book and tended to prattle on about things that upset her.

And there had been many things upsetting her lately.

"Or is it what he *didn't* do?" Derrick studied her closely, leaning in and getting in her face. "Hmm? Which is it?"

In a lonely voice, she said, "Braiden's secretary told me that he's extending his business trip a few more days."

"Typical." Derrick put one hand on his hip; the other hand, still holding the thermometer, waggled the device in the air. "You can do better than that jerk."

"He's not a jerk." The pit of her stomach twisted as she once again defended her fiancé. "He's sweet when we're alone."

Derrick's face pinched. "Hard to be alone when the man works late most nights and travels so much."

Braiden left last Tuesday. It would be ten days by the time he got back. "You don't know him as I do."

"I sure don't. The men in my life would never ignore me." Derrick's hand waved across his body in a Vanna White impression. "I'm too much man." He then stared at Kacie with a critical eye. "You're too much woman, Luv. You need a man who appreciates you."

A sad chorus repeated in her head. One she had heard too many times. "I'm happy with Braiden."

"If I knew any straight men, I'd set you up in a heartbeat." He studied her hair and added, "Maybe after a new hairstyle, some fresh clothes...." He leaned in. "Some makeup."

3

"I don't want to be set up." Nobody understood that she was already in her late twenties. Her life plan—the one she'd made when she was a teenager—was off course. She wanted to succeed in business by twenty–five, married by twenty–eight, and having her first child by thirty.

Ultimately, she wanted two or three kids.

And what was this about not wearing makeup? She'd applied some this morning. She liked the no–fuss, natural style with a ponytail updo. Besides, her glasses usually covered up any eye makeup she put on.

"So tell me, what makes Braiden so exceptional that you're willing to put up with his crap." Derrick lifted his hand. "And don't say the man is good in bed. I've seen that boy dance."

Sex? Her downstairs felt like cobwebs and mothballs. Two months had passed since Braiden had touched her, but she did not share that fact with anyone. She hoped the conversation would end, but then Derrick robotically swiveled his hips.

"Like. A. Stick. Up. His. Butt." His legs twisted ungracefully, and then he let out a shudder.

She couldn't help but laugh. Moving a step away from him, she hoped the conversation would end.

His eyebrow rose, and he touched her arm, stopping her mid-step. "Well?"

The answers were always the same. "Braiden's handsome, successful, rich…" she said, counting on her fingers.

Derrick's eyes narrowed. "What about how much you love him or how much he loves you? They weren't listed in the top three answers there, Luv."

She felt backed into a corner. She didn't like the feeling.

"I wasn't going in any order," she said, her voice defiant and strong. She had invested five years with Braiden, and she didn't want to start over with someone else—that was reason number one if she went in order. Besides, where would she find the time to date?

Braiden had swept her off her feet in graduate school. His magnetic personality had charmed her, and he had doted on her every whim. Their mature relationship had transitioned into one of comfort and security. There was nothing wrong with that.

"So why is his extended absence a problem? He's already been gone about a week." Derrick's eyes widened, followed by a look of pity. "Do you think he's cheating on you?"

The air left the room, and her lungs deflated. The insecurity she sensed made her feel the heat in her flushed cheeks. Braiden's potential cheating remained at the forefront of her mind lately, especially with his long work hours of late. But he didn't seem like the type. The walls pushed in. She squeaked out, "Of course not."

"Then why…?"

She took in a deep breath and let it out slowly. "Because my high school reunion starts this Friday."

Shame grew within her, slimy and thick, making it hard to breathe. She wanted to scream, *"Because Braiden said he'd be here,"* or *"Because he's missed so many other important things over the last five years,"* or even, *"Because if he cared for me, he'd know how important this reunion is to me."*

Instead, she walked to the hand sanitizer unit on the wall and squished out a ball of gel into her hands.

"You've been talking about this reunion for the last two months," Derrick said, his voice opinionated and shrill—sounding. "Some beach shindig and something at the Hilton?"

She shrugged and looked at the floor. "There's a get—together on Friday at the Leaning Pine. Then on Saturday, we have a barbecue at the beach, and then the Hilton on the big night."

"Your man can't take a hint."

She smeared the gel over her fingertips and palms, noting how dry her hands felt because of her profession. She had attended every dance during high school alone, and every party—even the graduation shindig at the end of her senior year. She wouldn't be the same non—datable girl she was in high school—she couldn't.

"I'm not going to the reunion alone. I'll skip it. Besides, Braiden always says to put the past behind us and move forward. Going to the reunion is…." She paused, looking for the right word and finally settling on the word Braiden had used. "…stupid."

"Stupid things are worth doing, girl." The grin that spread across Derrick's face—impish and devious—told her he had a plan.

His plans rarely ended well.

His eyes lit up. "You have a few days. You should get a new hairstyle, a sexy—as—hell dress, and at least go to that party at the Hilton like you own this town."

Her hairstyle had remained the same since middle

school. A sexy dress? Blue jeans and a T-shirt seemed more her style. "I don't think so."

"Build the life you want, Kacie. Don't settle for what is easy."

2
_____

G reg Bisset sat on the corner of his bed, staring at his phone as a tingle of pride radiated within him. The bank app showed the transfer of funds he had been waiting for.

He couldn't remember the last time he had been this happy.

"The sale is final. I now own my parent's old house, the home I grew up in." He glanced up from the phone and stared at Ashley, his lips curled into a proud smile.

"Uh-huh." She walked across the apartment's bedroom, holding a dress in front of her. She stopped in front of a full–length mirror. "God, I hate everything I own."

"Did you hear…?" he asked, turning the app around so she could see the bank statement.

Ashley threw the dress onto the floor and stormed into the walk-in closet, only to return with another outfit. She twirled it around, halfway dancing in front of the mirror before that frock met the same fate as the first.

While she swore in the closet, he glanced at the app

again. It also showed the automatic child support payment to his ex-wife. The amount was more this month since he also paid for his son's karate lessons and his daughter's ballet classes. His ex-wife called it "buying your child's love."

Buying their love? Since moving thirty minutes away from them, he had only seen his kids twice this year. Father's Day and Christmas.

The little time he got with them wasn't enough, but he couldn't help that his last job had taken him out of town for business. He was doing his best, even accepting a permanent position in his old hometown to see them more often.

He inwardly sighed. His children, now eight and six, called him by his first name and not Daddy these days. The oldest had started doing it nearly a year ago. That's when Greg noticed them moving apart even more.

"Greg! I swear you have no idea how to focus," Ashley said, her voice becoming so booming and loud that she woke their sleeping dog, Skipper, who began to bark.

She threw the dress she held down on the bed where Greg sat. "That damn dog."

Greg tapped his leg. "Come here, boy."

Skipper stopped his barking and obediently jumped onto the bed, tail wagging, wanting to cuddle.

"See? The training classes are working. You certainly can teach an old dog new tricks." Greg rubbed Skipper behind the ears. "You're a good boy."

Ashley scowled and gave him a sneer that only a teacher catching you misbehaving could pull off. "I don't know why you took in such a beast."

He wasn't sure if an eight–year–old, midsized golden retriever mix could ever be called a beast, especially when he licked you nonstop and loved on you. "Skipper got startled, that's all.

"...maybe even the king of the beasts...." Ashley continued, muttering to herself.

Skipper had been a spur–of–the–moment decision, one that Greg would never regret. The dog enjoyed hiking with him, curling up in his lap, and always seemed eager to hear about his day.

Greg rubbed the dog's ears and realized there were many benefits of a dog over an upset girlfriend.

Ashley stamped her foot and glared at him. "Yes, or no?"

He needed to pay more attention to her daily rants. "Whatever you want, sweetheart," he said politely to avoid further argument.

"Whatever." Ashley rolled her eyes and picked up the dress from the bed. "What do you think of this dress for Saturday night? I finally found the perfect outfit for the party at the Hilton."

He stared at the dress, which was low–cut in all the right places, and higher-cut in others. It looked perfect and was apparently new since he felt confident that he'd never seen her wear it before. He saw no tags, though, so he figured she had bought it specifically for the reunion. She had probably performed the entire closet tantrum just to cover up her shopping spree.

And if she needed to hide the purchase, how much did the dress cost?

"So this is the dress for Saturday." She placed it next to

another outfit on the bed. "This outfit will be for Friday night, and the shorts outfit for the barbeque Saturday afternoon."

This thing would take up the entire weekend. "You sure you want to go both Friday and Saturday?"

Her look told him he was being stupid. Of course, she wanted to do all the events. "Whatever you want is fine." He glanced at the bank app again.

Damn. The outfits must have been credit card buys—with *his* credit card.

Ashley was the beautiful cheerleader he'd never gotten a chance to date in high school, and she was still a size six with dynamite curves today. High–maintenance and in love with his bank account, but why should he complain? Showing up with her on his arm would make all the guys in the old clique jealous as hell. Maybe then, nobody would notice his failed marriage and the two children who never wanted to see him.

His lips parted into a devilish grin. "The outfits are perfect."

3

_____

"You're going to be fine, boy," Greg said in a soothing voice as he petted Skipper, who hid under his chair.

The exam room reassuringly smelled of antiseptic. The place looked clean, but he should have done more research on this vet clinic. The building was located a few blocks from his new house, but with no patients sitting in the waiting room on a Saturday morning, just how good of a clinic could it be?

A knock sounded on the interior door, followed by a man entering.

"I'm Derrick. This must be our new patient, Skipper."

Greg stood and shook the man's hand while Skipper continued to cower.

The vet tech held out his hand and allowed the dog to smell him. Next, he gently patted the dog's ears and coaxed him from under the chair. "Poor baby seems scared."

"I need to set up a new patient profile for him," Greg

answered. "Nail trimming and anal gland expression, as well."

Before leaving the room to get the doctor, Derrick filled out the paperwork with the usual information—what food the dog ate and how often he was fed, exercise habits, etc. The basic questionnaire seemed thorough, but Greg reserved making a final judgment on the place until he met the veterinarian.

"Super cutie in room #1 for you," Derrick said when he found Kacie in the back office and handed her the chart.

"The new dog?" She took the paperwork and headed toward the door.

He touched his ring finger. "No. Single hot man alert. The dog is cute, too, though."

"Stop." Kacie opened the door to the exam room and walked in. "Hi. I'm doctor Kacie Preston—" She stopped her everyday introductory speech and stared at the man's familiar green eyes. Her heart fluttered, and her lips spread into a smile—toothy and wide. "Greg?"

"Kacie?" he said in a surprised, what–the–heck–are–you–doing–here tone.

She hadn't seen him since they attended Linwood High School, and the twinkle in his cool green eyes told her he remembered her. When he stood and stretched out his arms to hug her, she didn't hesitate.

The embrace appeared friendly, but then, they'd never dated. Being neighbors as kids, their mothers the best of friends, had caused a bond to form between them. They'd probably still be close if he hadn't moved away to college.

"I didn't know you were back in town. My mother told me years ago that you moved to California." Kacie set the chart down and allowed Skipper to smell her hand before petting him. "Practically as far as you can get away from Pennsylvania and still be in the continental United States."

"I moved back a couple of years ago." His gaze traveled from her head to her feet, and then back up to the ring on her hand.

"You look fantastic." He then pointed to the diamond. "I see you're married."

She held out her hand so he could see the ring. "Soon." She felt awkward presenting her hand to him. He wasn't a gushing girlfriend who'd swoon at the size of the diamond and ask for all the details. Greg had always been more... she didn't know the right word. Grounded? Secure? Not so easily impressed by huge rocks on a gold band?

"He's a lucky guy."

His voice sounded hushed, and his eyes twinkled. They twinkled the same way when she had told him in high school that she had made AP honors in science. The same way they had shone when she announced she was going into medicine. The same way they always did when he was happy for her.

"I wish you all the happiness in the world, Kacie."

She blushed. His voice sounded husky and deep, not the high–pitched timbre she remembered. His jawline had turned square and manly—the type that young boys grew into as they matured into their twenties and thirties.

She liked a strong—Superman–like—jawline. And had Greg grown taller since she last saw him?

Silence spread between them for a long, awkward minute, and Kacie could mentally hear the clock ticking in the dead lull.

She glanced at Skipper's chart. "He's roughly eight years old? Who was his previous vet?"

Greg's gaze now focused on his dog, who hid behind his legs. "I recently adopted him. I was volunteering on an adoption day, and he was the only dog without a forever–home. The shelter said it was his last chance to find a family before they," Greg leaned in and whispered, "euthanized him the next morning."

A bubbling hatred grew in the pit of her stomach, threatening to rush out in a scream. "I hate those places. They treat animals like objects." She set the chart down on the exam table with a thunderous thud. "I want to start my own animal shelter. No-kill."

He smiled and said, "That's a great idea, Kacie."

She knelt and held out her hand so Skipper could sniff it. Instead, he lifted his paw as though completing the 'shake hands' command.

"He's such a good boy," Greg said. "How could I not have taken him home and saved his life?"

How not, indeed. She wondered what other Superman qualities the man held.

4

Greg's day had taken a turn for the better.

Kacie held the same pretty girl–next–door appeal and heart of gold she had in high school and was willing to meet him for coffee once the clinic closed at 11 a.m. There was so much to catch up on, and bumping into her had been a fluke.

Or, as his mother would have said, it was fate.

Mom always had a special place in her heart for Kacie. She was like the daughter his mother never had. Greg still remembered Kacie walking around his living room in high heels for the first time, his mother having lent them to her for a dance in middle school.

And how many bake sales had his mother contributed to, with Kacie in the kitchen helping out? Too many to count.

After dropping Skipper off at his parent's empty old house, he drove down the familiar streets searching for a Starbucks. The place proved easy to find. The coffeehouse stood where the convenience store used to be—the place where he had worked during high school, where he had taken his first car for gas, and where his old pals used to hang out if they weren't at the bowling alley or the mall.

Wasted adolescence at the time, the good old days now.

The town had changed a lot in the past ten years. He really should have come home sooner.

It seemed odd to romanticize the tiny town now, especially after traveling for work, living in Europe for a brief time, and always longing for big–city life. Meeting an old friend for coffee should have felt like going backward, but it didn't.

It felt right.

Once at Starbucks, he saw Kacie across the room. Her white vet coat was gone, and she wore a blue summer dress that picked up the hue of her eyes and made them sparkle like sapphires—even from across the room.

Her hair remained up in a ponytail, the way he remembered it. *Sloppy bun and getting stuff done* was an old saying. It described the girls who were self–reliant and determined to get better grades.

Kacie had certainly fit the bill back then. Even today, with the black-rimmed, no-nonsense glasses she wore, she gave off a scholarly appearance—one filled with confidence.

She looked like someone comfortable in her own skin. Not someone pretending they weren't a hot mess—the way he usually felt. Sure, he succeeded in business, but his personal life had been in the crapper for years. Kacie looked self–confident, like she had taken on the world over the last ten years and had won.

"There you are," she said as she approached him and raised her arms for a hug.

The embrace seemed slightly awkward at first, but he settled into it and hugged her back warmly. Her hair still smelled like lilacs.

Years may have passed, but she remained the same person who had helped him through chemistry. She had been there during his breakup with his high school sweetheart during his senior year. And she had encouraged him to follow a business career when his father wanted him to become a mechanic in his shop.

Once they got their orders, they settled on a couch.

"I knew you would follow your dream and become a vet." He smiled at her, thinking of all her determination in high school. "You never had a dream you couldn't chase and catch."

The blush on her face was pure Kacie. She glanced away, not able to take the compliment. Facing how wonderful she was had always been a shortcoming she had. Now, thinking back on how strong of a woman she was, it was her only shortcoming.

"The vet clinic is doing okay, but I'd like to move it a little farther north. Maybe somewhere near Congress Street. The location would be better, and I could get a bigger place. I'd have to advertise more, but the effort would be worth it."

Just like her to think toward the future. She was such a planner.

"Anyway, when I first saw you, I figured you were visiting your parents," she said, changing the subject. "I didn't realize you had been back for a few years."

He pushed back the pain of what that move had done to his marriage. The endless fights, the selfish accusations, and the hateful resentment from his wife for what she called 'dragging her and the kids' across the United States for a move she never wanted.

"My company made me an offer to head up their Pennsylvania office," he said, settling on a safer topic than his marriage. "I rented a house about an hour away, but then my parents needed more help."

His mother was fairing rather well, but she was a good eight years younger than his father. Alzheimers was a horrible condition, and his mother had gotten to where she could no longer be his sole caregiver. "I helped them move into a retirement home several months ago."

"I keep forgetting you're the youngest of five kids."

A large family, with everyone scattered across the United States. Maybe because he was the baby of the family, he wanted to be here for his parents. "If I remember correctly, you're the oldest of three."

They exchanged family news, sharing what each of their siblings was up to until Kacie asked, "I heard your parents finally sold their house."

"I bought it." A proud smile crept across his face. He had purchased a house. He was growing up. Finally.

One eyebrow lifted and hid beneath her bangs. "You own the place?"

"They wanted to hold onto it, maybe even rent it out. But we came to an agreement." Another toothy grin spread across his face. "It's closer to my work than my apartment in the Cedar Bend suburb."

"How nice. At least I know one family in the neighborhood. My little brother is a senior this year."

A senior? He remembered the day Tommy was born. It didn't seem so long ago. Kacie had come over with her other sibling. The two had hung out in his basement, talking and watching movies until the family brought the baby home.

"Speaking of school," he said, changing the topic. "Are you going to the reunion?"

"Maybe." She glanced away and sighed. "If I go, it'd just be for the Saturday night event."

The sigh—heavy with despair—sounded familiar. Her expression became the same every time something frustrated her. Uncertain of what it could be, he noticed a massive diamond ring on her finger again. "Maybe I can meet your fiancé at the reunion."

An odd expression crossed her face, but she held up her hand as if the ring became a beacon. "He's a wonderful man."

"Congratulations." He felt happy for her, but an odd sensation tugged at his heart. Kacie was not his *safety woman*. No pact existed between them where if the two weren't married by a certain age, they would tie the knot. But, to him, there had always been an unspoken arrangement.

"I heard you're married."

His stomach flopped, not once, but twice. "Married and divorced."

A look of pity followed by a head nod came from her. It was the expression he usually received when he mentioned the divorce, but why did Kacie give it to him?

She was never one of the masses who didn't know him or care. This was Kacie.

"I have two great kids, and life is all right." The lie came smoothly. Not wanting to focus on his past failures as a father, he said, "I've been dating Ashley Lewis for several months. Do you remember her?"

He had rambled and talked a mile a minute with no shut–up valve since the minute they had sat down. Talking with Kacie had never felt awkward before, so why should it now?

Kacie's skin turned ashen, followed by a crimson red. "You're dating Ashley? The wannabe Queen Bee and Mia Franco's shadow during high school?"

Mia Franco was the leggy, blue-eyed blonde everyone wanted to date. She ruled the school as the number one mean girl on campus. Ashley did her best to fit into the tight click Mia ran in. She just wasn't that much of a bitch to become Mia's BFF.

Doing a mental check, Greg tried to remember any history between Ashley and Kacie. There had been a lot. It seemed so long ago, but judging from Kacie's distressed look, not all had been forgiven.

5

K acie drove straight home after her coffee date, skipping her regular Saturday errands. She just wanted to be alone.

Entering her home, the alarm unit sounded. She punched in the code and glanced around the sparsely decorated place. This was Braiden's house. Clean and nearly showroom perfect. A few knick knacks here and there were hers, but this wasn't her home, even though she had lived in it for the last three years.

Three years of not paying rent or a mortgage. She sank the extra money into the vet clinic, but was it worth the price? Loneliness tugged at her heart, and she closed her eyes, focusing on the faces of the animals she had fostered and cured over the years.

It was definitely worth it.

But now she had a more significant problem than an absent fiancé or living in a place that felt like a hotel room. Once she'd discovered that Ashley Lewis would be on

Greg's arm at the reunion, Kacie said 'she wouldn't miss the event for the world'.

Wouldn't miss going to it? Greg would expect her to attend the reunion with her fiancé, and, once again, there'd be no one with her at the big dance.

She threw her purse down on the kitchen table and took a seat. She'd always thought Greg had better taste than Ashley Lewis. The train wreck of a woman had been a bitch in high school.

Back in the day, Ashley had kept Kacie off the cheerleading squad, cheated off her algebra work, and made fun of her nearly every chance she got. Worst of all, she had attended the prom with one of Kacie's friends—the one who'd been Kacie's safety net for a prom date.

It wouldn't have been so bad if Ashley hadn't told the entire school about the arrangement and humiliated Kacie in the middle of the gym—the same room where the prom would have been held if it hadn't flooded.

She thought back to prom night. The flooded gym caused the prom to be held on the drenched football field. Jordan Mitchell, the quarterback and captain of the team, and the rest of the players were indeed in their element. Jordan and Mia danced all night. Since Kacie's heels had dug into the turf and she had found it difficult to dance, she and Greg sat in the bleachers with friends and talked all night.

They had talked about college and their futures. She only wished she had told him then how much he had meant to her.

And now he was back in her life, but he was with Ashley.

Taking her phone from her purse, Kacie went on Facebook and searched for Ashley. The woman had never married, had no kids, and hadn't gained an ounce. She still looked like a doll with the perfect hard body, beautiful blonde hair, and a designer wardrobe.

According to social media, Ashley worked at the local newspaper in their advertising department. It came as no surprise to Kacie. Seems Ashley was the one who'd messed up all the advertisements for the veterinary clinic —even misspelling the address in one ad.

Kacie knew it had been no accident. Ashley hated Kacie like she hated all the girls at school who weren't in her somewhat Queen Bee clique. She also hated anyone who lived north of Hyde Park Street, where the wealthiest families lived.

Kacie went to her social media site and typed: *Looking forward to my high school reunion. It should be fun.*

Even reading the words didn't convince her, but she still posted it—making the action her final decision to go to the stupid event—at least the big event on Saturday night.

Glancing at years' worth of posted images, she realized she still looked the same. Holly Hobby–ish. Cute with no chance of happiness.

She grabbed her phone and dialed Derrick. "Want to be my date next Saturday night?"

"It's a beautiful day, Skipper."

Greg got the dog from the car and walked the short

distance to the dog park. Letting the furry baby off his leash, Skipper took off running and joined the other dogs in play.

"Skipper is adjusting to his new home." Ned took a sip of his coffee and pointed at his collie. "Copper enjoys his company."

The two dogs chased each other at top speed, and a bubbling burst of happiness overcame Greg. "Skipper was saved. Every day is a blessing."

"A blessing to you both," Ned said. "Copper is a rescue, as well. He means so much to me; I can't even begin to tell you. Many people want purebreds or tiny puppies. They don't understand the joy a mature dog needing a home can bring to them."

Many people didn't. Greg knew little about Ned, other than that he worked at some social media company, but he liked the man. He seemed hard–working and appeared to know what was important in life.

"Skipper just had a checkup. Kacie told me that he's in excellent shape. Maybe even a little younger than I thought. He's only about six or seven years old."

"Look at him,"—Ned tapped Greg on the shoulder —"you'd swear he was a puppy."

"Kacie took a shine to him. She kept petting him and calling him a good boy."

A puzzled expression crossed across Ned's face. "I thought you were dating a woman named Alice or something."

"Ashley."

"Right." Ned nodded. "And Ashley doesn't like Skipper."

Brick–by–brick, the wall grew stronger. Not that their relationship had seemed perfect to begin with. "She's still upset that I adopted him. I mean… I told her that I wanted to get a dog. I even asked her to come by on adoption day to meet him before I saved him."

"Is she allergic to dogs? Or is she just a cat person?"

Greg let out a slightly nervous chuckle, wishing it was something so simple. "Nothing like that."

"She doesn't like the breed of dog?"

"She hates dogs, period." The truth was hard to admit, but there it was. "Skipper can't do anything right. He gets into the trash, he barks too much, and the other day, he chewed up one of her shoes."

"Did you get him into that training class I told you about?"

"Yes. I hope that Ashley can see how much Skipper is changing. He had been a neglected dog for many years. He was a good ten pounds underweight when the shelter found him."

Greg thought back to how thin his little buddy had been. His ribcage showed through his skin, and his beseeching eyes had begged for help. "Kacie said he's a healthy weight now."

"Who is Kacie?"

A tingle of excitement filled him as an image of Kacie appeared in his mind. "She's Skipper's new vet. I knew her in high school, and she immediately remembered me."

Ned snapped his fingers and pointed at Greg. "That's right. You have your reunion coming up soon. It looks like you got a jump on the event by bumping into her. Maybe it was fate that Skipper needed a checkup."

Fate? Or just a fluke? Right now, Greg leaned more toward the former. Skipper would be in excellent hands with Kacie as his doctor.

"It was exciting to see her. She hasn't changed a bit." A smile broke across his face. "She always loved animals and had planned on becoming a vet one day." He let out a slight chuckle. "She was always so determined with her goals. I'm not surprised that she became a doctor and set up her own vet clinic."

"Kacie sounds great."

Greg thought back to his teenage days. She had been in the background for some events and in the spotlight for others. No matter what was going on, she was always there. At first, with their mothers being best friends, they were forced to have playdates. But those early days passed quickly, and then they hung out together out of true friendship. "She always watched my back and knew me better than I knew myself."

"Not that it's my place, but why are you and Skipper with the dog hater? Especially since Kacie seems perfect?"

Kacie? Kacie was his friend, not a potential love interest. "She's like a sister, or at the very least, a cousin."

"That's a shame," Ned said.

Kacie would make a wonderful wife and mother. He had always known that. By watching her babysit her younger siblings and take on so much responsibility at an early age, anyone could see that she'd become a Wonder Woman type of female.

So loving and compassionate.

Someone you could spend your life with and know where you stood.

The air turned thin, and he found it hard to breathe. Kacie *was* perfect. She had always been perfect. She understood his ups and downs and had been his personal cheerleader for years. Their friendship had only been torn apart due to their physical distance.

Could she be the one?

No. One major obstacle existed. She was engaged.

6

Greg didn't understand women.

It wasn't a big secret. Most men didn't. But Ashley accentuated the difference between the genders exponentially, making everything so much more complicated than it needed to be.

"Do you like this dress?", "Does this dress make me look fat?", "Should I put on a different set of earrings?", ...

He knew her not to be an insecure woman. She fished for compliments at every turn, taking them greedily while dishing out enough of the *"Are you really going to wear that outfit tonight? You look like a waiter..."* remarks.

He had hoped the ego–feeding and passive-aggressive comments would stop in the car, but he wasn't that lucky of a man.

"Circle back around. I'm sure there's a parking spot closer," Ashley said in between applying lipstick with the help of the passenger seat mirror. She rolled her eyes after he drove over another bump in the road. "My grandmother can drive smoother than this," she muttered.

He wanted to say something, but the smear of lipstick on her cheek was rewarding enough. Glancing down another row of parked cars, he said, "I told you we should have arrived earlier. Looks like the place has a couple of events tonight."

Her sharp tongue accompanied her cold gaze. "You never show up to an event on time. Only losers do that."

"It's 8:11 pm," he said, staring at the clock on the dashboard. "We're an hour late."

She put away her lipstick and closed the car's folding mirror. "Anyone who is anybody is only now showing up." She glared at him, practically sizing him up. "Trust me. I know."

His jaw tensed. How is it that high school holds the fastest key to dividing people into the essential "Breakfast Club" categories? Prom queen, geek, jock, misfit, or outlaw. He'd say there were more pigeonholes for people to fit into, but as a geek/jock person, he knew his old role well.

"If you're the first to arrive, you can't make a grand entrance. And I didn't spend this much money on this dress to not be noticed."

Her voice softened as she finished her sentence, as though she didn't want to admit how much she had spent. Like the credit card bill wouldn't tell him soon enough.

Her hand brushed his leg in a fake caress, and her lips curled into a plastic smile. "I just want to make this night special," she said, her eyes holding the true meaning of the word *special*.

It meant 'forget about the cost of the dress, and you'll get birthday–type of sex tonight.' He could live with that, but just how much had she spent on this weekend's outfits?

It was probably a hefty amount. He knew her need to impress all the people she hadn't bothered to keep up with since graduating. He just didn't understand it. Great parking spot and frugal spending be damned. A grand entrance was *much* more critical.

Her hand still lay on his thigh. It remained a little longer than usual when she wanted her way, and she knew how to play him. The sooner they got the night over with, the better.

He drove down another row of cars. "I'm not finding any spot to…."

"Drop me off at the front door," she said, removing her hand and cutting him off. "Then you can park the car."

"Fine. I'll drop you off at the main entrance." He rounded the corner and took her to the rounded drive.

"I'll see you inside." She got out of the car and closed the door. She then walked determined and sure into the building, never looking back—and there went any chance of him walking in with her on his arm and impressing the old gang.

His shoulders slumped, and he felt a loss. Maybe he did understand the need to make a grand entrance. He was more like Ashley than he wanted to admit.

And that was definitely something to work on.

After several minutes, he found a parking spot and walked into the Leaning Pine resort. A sign for Linwood High School class reunion sat just inside the main entrance with the name and an arrow pointing to a private party room.

He followed the signs and the music, and entered the room. No fan fair. No special entrance. No adoring fans. No grand entrance.

He walked in without notice. Just like in high school, but with one significant difference. Linwood didn't have a bar.

"Scotch. Neat." He placed a twenty on the bar and scanned the room.

Ashley stood across the room, looking stellar in the new dress. He eyed her from head to toe, pride swelling inside of him. Whatever the outfit had cost, it was worth the price. He grinned from ear–to–ear. Having a trophy like her on his arm would make him the envy of every man in the place.

Ashley talked with another woman and let out a fit of laughter. Greg would have said that the woman made a witty comment, but he recognized Ashley's fake cackle. It held a touch of nervousness mixed with self–doubt. The phony smile she wore was a telltale sign she wanted to impress the woman she was having a discussion with, but, based on the way she gulped her drink, she was failing at it.

The woman looked familiar, and he racked his brain trying to place who she was. She had attended their high school, but with nearly 150 graduating seniors in their class, it proved hard to remember everyone.

He gathered his change from the bartender and then studied the green-eyed beauty, only to confirm what he suspected. She was Sasha Monroe. She had performed in most school plays and musicals and became a somewhat famous actress.

At least, that was the rumor. He hadn't bothered to keep up, but evidently, Ashley had.

He let out a chuckle. Sasha looked trapped and eager to escape from Ashley's clutches. He would have considered helping Sasha out, but they had never been friends. She was too busy making most of the high school boys feel inferior to Jordan Mitchell, the football team captain—the one person she had wanted to date throughout all of high school. Of course, he was already dating Mia Franco, the head cheerleader.

God. Five minutes into the reunion and he was already caught up in the drama of yesteryear.

"Oh my gosh! Greg?"

Greg turned around and was face–to–face with a tall blond man. Even though he looked familiar, Greg had to read his name tag to know who the man was.

"Grady Cox? Is that you?"

Grady leaned in to give Greg a half-hearted–manly hug. It felt odd initially, but Greg figured this would be the first of many hugs for the evening. "It's been a long time."

He studied his old friend. Many people peak in high school, but that wasn't the case for Grady, who was constantly teased by his name back in the day. The man looked better now than ten years ago when he was a tall, lanky kid who sat at the nerd table in the cafeteria. He had filled out and was a handsome man with a square jaw. "How've you been?"

"I can't complain." He reached into his pocket and pulled out a business card. "I'm a newspaper editor in

Maryland." He handed Greg his card and added, "I heard you were back in town for good."

Greg stared at the business card. Leave it up to a man who worked in the print industry to carry such an outdated form of connecting with others. Greg had planned to capture people's contact info on his phone, but he stuffed the card into his back pocket.

"I moved back a while ago. How's the newspaper business these days? Must be tough with all the electronic news out there."

"You'd be surprised," Grady said. "We have electronic newspapers and even some electronic magazines, but the paper industry isn't as dead as everyone thinks it is."

Grady had been in Greg's homeroom and several other classes. A good study buddy, a good helpful friend, and an overall good guy. The type of person who got tortured a lot for being smart, but hit upon for any tutoring whenever someone needed it. "I'm glad to hear that you're doing well. You deserve it."

Grady raised a bill and caught the bartender's attention. "Beer, whatever you have in a bottle, is fine." He then returned his attention to Greg. "What are you doing these days?"

"I'm the Northeast Director of Research at Lermer Industries," he said, his voice filled with pride. "I'm heading up a new project and…" he noticed Grady's gaze traveling the room as he continued to explain his job. "It's more exciting than how it sounds."

"Same with the newspaper biz," Grady said, smiling. "Most people think I'm correcting the articles written by the Lois Lanes of the world. There is so much more to the newspaper industry than that. I mean, the paper makes quite a bit of money through advertising alone, and the marketing efforts are state of the art."

Advertising? Greg tilted his head and asked, "Is your marking all print advertising?"

"Mostly." Grady took a swig of his beer. "We do run ads in our electronic publications."

Greg stood taller. "Any of them local ads?"

"Some. Why?"

Opportunity knocked on the door, and Kacie was nowhere in sight. "My friend Kacie is looking for local advertising, and she might be interested in talking to you if you know of any local editors." He glanced around. "She said she probably wouldn't show up tonight, though."

"Kacie Preston?"

"You remember her?"

He held up his hand to about the same height Kacie was. "Really adorable, sandy brown hair," he gestured with his hand, "hair always up in a ponytail or bun?"

"That's her."

"Weren't you two an item throughout all of high school?"

Greg's eyebrows furrowed. "No, we were just friends."

"Really? I thought for sure you two were dating." He shook his head. "The two of you were so good together, I just assumed."

He had definitely spent a lot of time with Kacie during those four years, and now, looking back, he had been blind. She was always at his side, helping him with homework, working with him at the local grocery store after school, and even attending every basketball game to cheer him on. Not to mention all the times he stood by her when her mother was sick with cancer.

They had been good together.

But now, she was engaged.

And he was a divorced man whose ex-wife had a laundry list of reasons why he was a terrible husband.

Not that he hadn't tried his hardest to please the woman.

Ashley walked to the bar, so Greg caught her by the arm and pulled her close, his arm snaking around her slender waist. He wasn't a complete loser. He had a hot woman in his life today. "Honey, do you remember Grady."

She stared blankly at Grady's face and then read his name tag. "So nice to see you again," she said, holding out her hand while her eyes scanned the room. Her tone of voice told Greg she had no idea who Grady was, and her stiff body told him she was upset and didn't want to be bothered.

"I think that's Mia." She finished shaking Grady's hand and waved to the ex-head cheerleader. She left without saying goodbye, and Greg felt a prickly feeling on the back of his neck. She had made him look like a fool.

"Was that Ashley...?" His voice trailed off, and his face pinched trying to remember her last name.

"Ashley Lewis." Greg stood taller and tried to salvage his pride. "I've been dating her for several months."

Grady's lips pursed in a judgmental way. "You and Ashley?" He took another sip of beer. "I never saw you with someone like her."

Hours had passed. The music still played, but the bar had shut down. Greg had been ignored by Ashley long enough and was ready to leave.

"There you are," Ashley said, walking up to the table where he sat. "Where have you been?"

"Here. Alone." He didn't know what else to say. She had spent time with everyone else except for him. What was the point of showing off a beautiful babe if she treated you like a piece of furniture?

"You've been drinking." Her expression became dismissive. "Everyone important is gone. Besides, there'll be plenty of time tomorrow to talk."

He glanced up and noted that most people had left, the 'important' ones and everyone else. She was probably always a snob, but the reunion brought it out more. Her behavior wasn't attractive.

"I'll drive us home tonight."

He stood and took a deep breath, smelling the alcohol. "Thanks."

She hooked her arm in the crux of his. "In case you're curious, my friend Lily and I have worked everything out."

"Worked what out?" He hadn't talked to Ashley in over an hour, Kacie hadn't shown up, and all he wanted to do was go home. He didn't even know who Lily was.

Her frown deepened. "The king of beasts idea, of course."

They walked out of the room and down the hallway to the front entrance of the Leaning Pine. "What are you talking about?"

"God, you never listen." She rolled her eyes. "Never mind."

His wife always said he didn't listen. Maybe it was true, not that he wanted to admit she was right about anything. "No. Tell me. I'm really interested."

"It's nothing." She held him tighter as they made their way out the door and to the parking lot. "Tomorrow, there is a barbeque at the lake." Her eyes lit up from the moonlight. "Should be a lot of fun. Remember all the good times down there?"

He really didn't. The Straights, where the popular kids hung out, wasn't his old haunt. Ashley may have been on the outskirts of acceptance by the "in" kids at school, but he certainly wasn't. He and his friends usually hung out at the bowling alley or the mall.

"The barbeque is from 11 am to 4 pm tomorrow."

That time sounded familiar. Familiar in an 'I'm already booked' sort of way. "Is tomorrow Saturday?"

"Yes."

He mentally went through his day planner and came up with the answer. "We can't go."

"What?"

"My daughter's dance recital is tomorrow afternoon. I told her we'd be there."

"I can't miss the barbeque." She looked around at the cars in the lot. "Where the hell did you park?"

He pointed down a row of cars. "It's important that you go to the recital with me. We already told my daughter we'd go, and we don't want to disappoint her."

"It's just a dance. She'll have more."

He had tried to attend every school function, every day

camp, and every recital since the divorce—attempted to attend, not that he actually made it to them. Goodness knows he had already lost too much with his children and didn't want to miss out on another event. "I'd like for you to go with me to see my daughter dance."

She held up her phone. "Just record it. I can watch it later."

"It's not the same."

She got him into the car. Before she closed the door, she said, "Let's go home. I have a terrible headache and want to get some sleep."

7

S aturday night arrived faster than Kacie had expected. She had kept her vet clinic open until 11 am but then had to run errands all over town to prepare for tonight.

It was almost not enough time.

She closed her car door and walked alone to the Hilton entrance. Braiden should have been here to take her to the dance. Hell. He should have been here Friday night for the meet-and-greet and also this afternoon for the barbeque. But, he had to work. He always worked, which should be a positive trait in a future spouse, but anger still built up inside of her. The reunion was just one more disappointment for her.

And there had been quite a few disappointments lately.

Walking into the hotel unescorted reminded her of all the dances at high school, where she had entered the gym alone. Even when she had driven to events with Greg, she had still been alone.

He had never seen her as anything but the geeky girl–next–door. The kid with all the chemistry answers who could help him study. Did he even know how much she detested basketball?

No. She had kept everything in, not telling him her feelings. She had been a wallflower, never really fitting in anywhere.

But today, she didn't need to sit at the popular girls' table, have the jocks like her, or fear going down the hallways where the potheads sold weed. There was no locker with her lock on it anymore.

She was a successful veterinarian. Even if her business wasn't thriving and she was still single and childless, she still had much to be proud of.

She strutted into the grand hotel, her high heels clicking against the hard marble. Unfortunately, she wasn't sure where to go but then saw a sign. A green and gold banner with a Royal Lion and the name Linwood High caught her attention. Beside it stood a navy and gray banner with a cougar and the name of their rival high school, St. Martin's Academy.

The private boarding school's choice of venue didn't surprise her. The Hilton was one of the nicest hotels in town. Rival school or not, there were only so many weekends in the summer to choose from to hold a reunion.

Derrick stood near her high school's banner, looking like a million dollars. She had seen him in his vet clinic smock and blue jeans just a few hours ago. Now, his expensive suit fit perfectly, and the man cleaned up so well that a surge of pride shot through her. He was her date for the reunion. Heads would turn and take notice.

Derrick's eyes lit up when he saw her. "Damn, girl."

A smile cut across her face. That was all she needed to hear. "You look amazing yourself."

"I'm glad you told me the name of your high school. Looks like two reunions are going on."

"St. Martin's Academy is a private boarding school and our rival." They walked into the Linwood reunion ballroom and to the table with the name tags.

"High school. No matter which one you attend, they all look the same." Derrick put on his name tag, the one with Braiden's name on it with a big red *guest* written across the bottom. "My reunion was last year, but I didn't go."

"Why not?"

He gave her an are–you–kidding–me look. "My straight-laced school would freak out if I brought a date. I'd probably get kicked out before hitting the dance floor."

She knew Derrick had not yet embraced his lifestyle until going to college. He had been from a ritzy neighborhood, and they wouldn't have accepted him ten years ago. But things had changed since then. There was more acceptance these days.

"Lockers, classrooms, and hallways. I guess they all look the same, and one reunion is the same as the next," Kacie said, trying to support him.

She didn't recognize the two people handing out name tags at the table. They appeared young and were probably students—most likely volunteering for honor society or some other credit. She had done the same at that age, so it'd look good on her college applications.

"Everyone seems to be in the ballroom." She glanced down the hallway to where all the colorful signs—all in their school colors—indicated the event would be. Where everyone she'd graduated with would be.

Including Greg.

Handsome neighbor and best friend, Greg.

Years had passed since she had seen him, but time had treated him well. He had a brawnier build than in high school, with muscles to spare. Apparently, he worked out regularly, probably taking Skipper on many hikes.

Hearing the rhythmic tune of what she thought might be a slow dance coming from the ballroom, she thought back to Greg's tall frame and muscular arms. Her lips curled into a smile as she thought about dancing with him, huddled up next to his chest and feeling his arms around her.

He had looked gorgeous in his T-shirt and shorts last week, but tonight, he'd probably be dressed in a suit. Perhaps a gray suit with a power tie, wearing a masculine cologne that could draw any woman in and promise to consume them whole.

Butterflies in her stomach threatened to fly up and out of her mouth. What was she doing? Fantasizing about a man who was currently dating one of the bitchiest girls from their graduating class?

She was happy with Braiden. The two shared a mature relationship filled with mutual respect and understanding.

"You ready to go in?" Derrick asked.

"Sure." She put on her name tag that sported her maiden name. It proved that she'd never gotten to walk down the aisle and say, "I do." She wasn't someone's wife. She wasn't anyone's mother. She was just someone who had remained stagnate since high school, most likely peaking the day she graduated.

A lonely thread tugged at her heart. Braiden should be here. His work was necessary as the data architect in a Fortune 500 company, but it shouldn't be the only thing in life. The first year or two with him had seemed like a honeymoon. They were always together, holding hands, talking, and making love. They had been inseparable.

Now, they were rarely in the same state as each other.

Derrick held out a crooked arm. "Let's do this."

She let out a sigh and took Derrick's offering. Over time, what she shared with Braiden turned into something more relaxed, comfortable, more... boring. It seemed to be the natural order for relationships.

Braiden made her feel safe. There had been no history with him, no friendship to ruin, and no risk of loss if things didn't go well.

"You have to move your feet if we're going to make it to that dance floor." Derrick glanced down and gave her a puzzled expression. "You doing okay?"

"I shouldn't have gone so short." She let go of his arm and fidgeted with her hands a moment before grasping his elbow again and beginning their trek to the dance. "It just doesn't feel natural."

"You look stunning in that dress." Derrick studied the light blue, spaghetti–strapped silk dress that clung in all the right places. "If you ask me, you could have gone shorter on that hemline and showed off more of your legs."

She did like the dress. The plunging neckline was too low, and the hem was too high, but she had to admit, she felt like a million dollars in it. The shoes pinched her feet, but some sexy shoes with killer high heels would do that.

"I'm talking about my hair." She brushed back her now wispy bangs and again stopped their trek to the ballroom. "I've never worn it so short before."

After she had cut it, the hairstylist had blown it dry in a sexy, come–hither look that Kacie thought was sassy. She'd sent a picture to Braiden, but he hadn't responded to say whether or not he liked it.

Which meant he probably hated it.

She'd had to buy hair gel and some curling brushes to attempt the same style at home, and she felt like she hadn't mastered the technique yet.

He studied her short hairstyle and smiled. "If you ask me, it makes you look ten years younger." When she grinned and shook her head, he added, "I'm serious. You should have gone short, sexy, and sassy years ago."

"You like it?"

He gave her his best are–you–kidding–me glare. "Honey, I'm even tempted by the way you look tonight, especially with the new contacts and not your bookworm glasses on."

Those words were what she needed to hear. Derrick was a good enough friend to tell her the truth and not trump up what he thought she needed to hear.

With her ego now boosted, Kacie was ready to walk into the room. She had only taken a few steps in that direction, hearing her high heels click on the tiled floor before she got sideswiped by someone from behind.

"Sorry. I didn't see you there."

Kacie turned to see who it was, but that soft and syrupy

voice was hard to miss. She could still hear it in the back of her mind on bad days, the days she knew the world had slapped her down for something.

Ashley Lewis stood in front of her. All five–foot–nine inches of her, with her slender body frame and luscious blonde hair. She looked as if she had stepped out of a salon where she had spent a week grooming for this event.

The near hit–and–run didn't surprise Kacie. Ashley never saw anyone unless her claws were out.

Ashley stared at Kacie's face, examining every inch. Finally, an eyebrow raised. "Holly? Right?"

She hadn't changed in all these years. "Holly Hobby" was the disparaging nickname Ashley had given her during their four years of high school because of her girl–next–door appearance and clothing. Evidently, the woman couldn't read a name tag, even when it was one foot from her face.

"You look so different." Ashley shook her head in disbelief.

Kacie pointed to her name tag. "I'm Kacie." She reached out her hand, but Ashley didn't offer hers.

"I must have you confused with someone else." She shifted the Wal–Mart bag in her hand and nearly dropped it. She sighed deeply and said, "Nothing is working tonight."

"What's not working?" Kacie asked.

Ashley plastered what appeared to be a fake smile on her face. "So nice that you're here tonight." She turned and continued the walk down the hallway. "I'll see you in the ballroom in a little while."

As they watched her walk away, Derrick asked,

"Please tell me the two of you were not BFFs in high school."

Kacie shook her head. "Quite the opposite." Her confidence felt shot after having seen her old nemesis. She was glad Derrick didn't ask about the *Holly* comment.

"Why is it that after all this time, I'm immediately brought back to my insecure teenage days and feeling useless? And her outfit? Did you see what she was wearing?"

"Don't worry about her."

Ashley's outfit could have had its fabric weaved by magical fairies, and her high heels were definitely designer. Feeling deflated like an ugly step–sister was easy to do with Ashley in the room.

"Now, none of that," Derrick scolded, obviously picking up on her mood change. "You're the star of the evening, and you're stealing this show."

8

G reg drove to the Hilton for the reunion. He no longer cared if Ashley hung on his arm or not. In fact, he didn't really care to go to the damn thing.

But Kacie had said she might be there.

And that was worth the drive over.

He parked his car and sat thinking. He wasn't sure what Ashley was doing and didn't care. She experienced another one of her fake headaches last night and then gave him the cold shoulder this morning as he fed Skipper his breakfast. The silent treatment continued until she left for the barbeque, and he also expected a frosty evening from her tonight.

But his daughter's dance recital had been fantastic. He sat through three hours of other kids dancing to see her on stage for five minutes and twenty–two seconds, but they were a good few minutes.

Her smile was priceless, and joining them for ice cream afterward felt right. He needed to spend more time with his kids. Needed to repair their relationship. And Ashley was not the answer.

She wasn't a good potential step–mother for his kids. He knew that. She was a good–time gal with no responsibilities or cares.

Initially, he was supposed to pick her up after exercising at the gym. But she had called and told him to meet her at the school instead. She mentioned needing something from Wal–Mart, but then she curtly cut off the conversation by saying she'd pick it up herself.

Her voice had reached the plaintive, shrilling wail of frustration. He had heard it once or twice, which meant that something wasn't working out the way she'd planned. A tantrum threatened to brew, but he didn't get to ask her what she was doing. Not that he really wanted to know.

She had said she would take care of Skipper. Giving him his dinner was unlike her, but he appreciated that she sometimes tried.

Which made him feel guilty. His mind was in a completely different place. It had been a week since he had seen Kacie, yet all he thought about was how she had slipped from his fingers.

He could have dated her in high school. He could have dated her in college.

But, no.

He couldn't get past seeing her as a friend. No, not as a friend, as a sister.

God, he had been stupid.

He exited the car and slammed the door shut. His old buddies from the basketball team were probably here, his former study partners… Kacie.

And Ashley waited for him inside. If he'd read her tone correctly over the phone, she was already upset. Showing up late would not make the situation any better.

He entered the hotel and got his name badge, noticing that Ashley's was missing from the table. She'd be in the ballroom waiting for him, her dance card no doubt filled, her expectations high of a perfect night.

"Greg?" a familiar voice sounded behind him.

Greg turned around and quickly smiled. He hadn't been the most popular guy in school, but to be recognized within the first two minutes of entering the building? He must have beaten some type of record.

The man had aged over the years but remained tall and lean. His hairline had traveled a bit north, and he wore a light gray suit, not the familiar basketball jersey Greg had usually seen him in. "Steve?" He hugged his old team member. "How are you doing?"

"Doing well." He balled up his fists and did a one-two gentle punch on Greg's arm. "You don't look too worse for wear."

The dark gray suit and power tie added to his confidence, but could only carry you so far. He wondered if Steve and the rest of the crew suspected what a mess his life had become. "I'm doing all right, I guess."

"All right?" Steve gave him an all-knowing smile. "Your mother bragged to everyone about you moving to Europe. She said…"

Greg nodded and listened to the regaling. On paper, his life sounded perfect.

"Where are my manners." Steve's arm snagged the

waist of a lovely blonde standing near him. "This is my wife, Carol."

Greg shook her hand, noticing her silky skin. She was sunshine fresh, the type of girl Steve had always pursued. She was also pregnant enough to pop. "Is this your first child?"

She rubbed her belly. "Number three."

"Wow. Three kids."

Steve proudly smiled. "Happy family life and healthy career in commercial real estate. I'm at the top of my game."

His grin showed his happiness. Greg guessed if the marriage were strong enough, a litter of kids would add to the blessing—especially with a good job and money coming in.

"What about you?" Steve asked. "Didn't I hear that you got married?"

Greg gave the typical I'm–a–statistic–of–divorce speech and shook off any further questions about his kids. Steve and Carol gave him the usual, that's–too–bad frowns, but Greg didn't go into any details. There was no reason to bring the mood down.

The longer he waited, the more he didn't want to walk into the ballroom—at least, not alone.

"I'm dating Ashley Lewis now." His voice sounded proud and confident.

Steve appeared deep in thought, and a moment later, he asked, "The cheerleader who was expelled for getting drunk with one of the math teachers?" He added, "Didn't she shave off the teacher's hair when she passed out?"

That was Ashley? He had nearly forgotten about that

incident. Now thinking back on the event, he remembered the story well. It didn't cast his date in the best of lights, so he said, "The teacher was fired. Ashley was only suspended."

Greg bumped into eight other friends, Coach Owens, and Ms. Lopez (his old Spanish teacher), before making his way to the beverage table.

He ordered a beer and surveyed the room. He figured they couldn't pack this room with more green and gold had they tried. Green tablecloths, green and gold balloons, and centerpieces... the place looked like a leprechaun convention with everyone spilling their pot of gold on the dance floor.

People milled about, but he didn't see Kacie anywhere. He didn't know everyone in his graduating class, which was just as well. Other than bumping into Steve, he wasn't enjoying the evening.

And he still hadn't found Ashley.

Walking around telling everyone you were dating the prettiest ex-cheerleader when she wasn't there smacked of pure fantasy. Back in the day, when he had grown into his awkward years of teenage acne, a cracking voice, and a scrawny body, no one would have believed he'd eventually date her.

Now, he couldn't even show her off.

People gathered in packs of two, each with a significant other in their lives.

And that's when he saw a vision of beauty. One woman

stood with her back to him. Her curvy figure, long legs, and stilt-like heels said she meant business. Her body resembled a perfect hourglass, and he wasn't sure if he had ever met someone with such proportions. It must be the old prom queen. He couldn't remember her name, but she —or was it the homecoming queen?—was fantasy–figure beautiful like this. Or at least she had been.

He wasn't the same nobody from high school, so he built up his courage to say hello. Hell, it was better than being a wallflower and standing at the bar.

Plus, his old buddy Steve was talking with her. Being happily married and a good father could give anyone enough confidence to speak to a pretty woman. There were no expectations, no hidden agendas, and no sexual innuendo.

If Steve knew the goddess, then there was a chance Greg did too.

Steve left, and she turned around and looked in Greg's direction. Her piercing blue eyes stared past him, not seeing him.

She looked so familiar, but he figured he would remember her had he gone to school with such a knockout. She had the reddest, poutiest, sexiest lips he had ever seen. And that haircut? Self–confident, beautiful women got away with boy–cut short styles. Like they knew they didn't need long tresses to get the attention of every man in the place.

It was sexy.

She was sexy.

Her dress showed off her firm body in ways that gave him small glimpses of flesh, but only enough to tease. The soft, supple, and flawless skin of her ample bosom overflowed the bodice of her dress. Slender legs peeked from the hem, just short enough to entice.

She radiated beauty.

As impure thoughts danced around in his mind, a man walked up to her with a glass of wine. A heartwarming smile crossed her face, and she glowed—as if she were in her element and nothing about the evening could upset her.

Naturally, she was taken. Beautiful women like that were always in relationships.

Greg stared at the man. He stood tall, had dark hair, and wore an expensive suit. What did this man have that Greg didn't?

Well, other than a sexy, girl–next–door hottie on his arm.

The woman's gaze wandered back in his direction, and a familiar smile greeted him. The curve of her cheekbones, the sparkle of her eyes, the slope of her neck, the arch of her brow... somehow, he knew her.

Greg blinked a few times and did a double–take. His heart lept into his chest, rattling so hard that his heartbeats echoed in his ears.

That smile. He had seen it after every birthday party, basketball victory, and significant life event. Bright and cheery, full of support and... love.

Kacie was the sexy woman.

The woman with the silky skin he wanted to touch.

The woman who had been the focus of every impure thought he had had over the last two minutes. Some things he had imagined... he was still thinking about them.

His mouth went dry and gaped open as she walked over to him.

Before he could utter a word, her arms wrapped around him, and she kissed him on the cheek. "I'm so glad you're here, Greg."

He pulled slightly away but still held onto her. "You look... your hair... you... "

She smiled and touched her new hairstyle. "I went with a change."

The man who followed her over now stood close to her. The badge held the name Braiden. He was a visitor tonight and not a former student, although he looked vaguely familiar.

He had to be Kacie's fiancé. Greg's competition.

9

"Greg, this is Derrick." Kacie smiled and gazed into Greg's green eyes. The eyes she knew she could get lost in. "Derrick, this is Greg. He's an old friend of mine."

Greg stood taller as he shook Derrick's hand. Greg's broad chest strained against the single-breasted gray suit jacket, buttoned and showing off his excellent figure. His face sported a scruffy, short beard, one that Kacie wanted to touch.

"Couldn't find your badge?" Greg pointed to Braiden's name on Derrick's name tag.

It felt like a knife jabbing into her chest. Showing up without her fiancé was terrible enough, but now she had brought a friend to the dance. She was pathetic. Like she needed a cousin to escort her somewhere because no one else would.

If only she could hari kari herself into oblivion.

"My fiancé, Braiden, couldn't make it." Years ago, she

would have told Greg all about her troubles, but not today. He was practically a stranger that she hadn't seen in ten years. A handsome stranger she hadn't stopped thinking about since he stumbled into her vet clinic—and her life—again. She hoped to let any mention of Braiden end.

"Her fiancé is on an extended business trip," Derrick said. "I'm a friend. I work with her at the clinic."

Greg's eyes lit up. "You took care of Skipper last week. I thought you looked familiar."

The two men smiled, then the conversation died, leaving the three with nothing to talk about and a stretch of awkward silence.

"We've had wonderful weather this week," Greg said. "I've taken Skipper on several long hikes."

"Oh? Where did you go?" Derrick asked.

Kacie couldn't listen to the boring conversation, so she drowned it out. The idle chitchat was killing her. Greg, who had been there for her the day her cat died, the day her heart had first been broken, and the day her mother was diagnosed with cancer, was now passing the time with small talk. Back in the day, she had only to look at him, and he could read her moods and know all her troubles.

Something in her life was missing during vet school. Now, looking into Greg's all-too-familiar face, she knew it had been him.

Next-door-neighbor Greg. Did he ever know about the crush she had had on him? How much she had wanted to go to the prom with him?

No. She didn't think he did. She had hidden her feelings too well. The few dates she had gone on as a teenager were poor attempts to move on as she watched his love life soar.

He had always been out of her league.

"I love the music they're playing," Derrick said. "But my knee has been bothering me the past few days. Greg, why don't you and Kacie dance?"

Derrick didn't have an issue lifting an eighty–pound dog earlier that day at the clinic. She was just about to ask him when he had hurt his knee when Greg's face lit up. First prize at a fair hadn't been offered, only a dance. A dance with her. Before she could say anything, Greg extended his hand, and she found herself reaching out to accept it.

"If you're sure you don't mind," he said, not even looking in Derrick's direction.

Kacie's hand felt soft and warm. It rested within Greg's hand and fit perfectly in his palm. He led her to the dance floor and must have walked past dozens of people, but he didn't notice any of them.

Standing in the middle of the floor, he turned to face her. She stood several inches shorter than he, even in her high heels, and he gazed into her blue eyes and familiar face.

She was the one who'd played Dungeons and Dragons with him, played video games with him, and never played any tricks. She had been honest in their friendship. She had always been there for him. And now, she was happy and engaged to be married.

Married to a man named Braiden.

What kind of stupid name was *Braiden* anyway?

A protective surge engulfed him. Braiden, whoever he was, had better treat her right. She deserved only the best.

Greg placed his hand on her back and leaned in for the slow dance. With his cheek next to her forehead, he no longer gazed into her eyes.

Just as well.

It felt awkward to hold her, strange to touch her, and disconcerting to have growing feelings for her.

Plus, it was awkward to know that she wasn't available.

He wasn't sure if he could look her in the eyes as he danced with her—his body mere inches from hers. Her rose–scented perfume tantalized his nose and drew him closer.

They danced to the old love ballad, ignoring everyone else around them. Inhaling deeply, he nuzzled his cheek closer to her soft, delicate neck. His lips brushed her tender skin.

"I've missed you," he whispered into her ear, realizing how true the statement was.

"I've missed you, too."

Holding her tight, he closed the small gap between them. The two swayed together in step with the tune, her warm breath brushing against his ear. A tingling sensation surged through him, arousing him.

This was Kacie. Someone he had known for most of his life. But it didn't matter. He closed his eyes and focused on how right it felt to hold her.

A jolt from his back forced his eyes open, and he spun around, dropping his loving embrace of Kacie.

Ashley poked him again. With a plastered fake smile, she said in a singsong voice that didn't match the hatred in her eyes, "There you are. I've been looking everywhere for you."

10

Greg left the ballroom and followed Ashley down the hall. The long strides she took in her high heels and the speed with which she walked told him one thing. She was pissed.

A virtual noose tightened around his neck. He had only himself to blame. She would be angry about this for a long time, yet he'd done nothing to deserve her wrath.

Well, almost nothing.

Shit.

He couldn't blame Ashley for being upset with him. While dancing with Kacie, he'd nearly kissed her neck.

Stupid. Stupid. Stupid.

Without slowing her pace, Ashley turned so she could glare at him. Her reddened face cast an evil, witch-like appearance across her face. "You embarrassed me."

"I danced with an old friend," he said, preparing for the fight and stopping her from continuing down the hallway.

"When you're at a reunion and my date, it's not just a dance. I'm glad no one important noticed."

So it really was all about her. He could try and explain everything until he turned blue in the face, but instead, he said, "Nothing happened."

"Well, of course, nothing happened," she said in an icy tone. "It still looks bad. But I'm sure it won't happen again."

And that's when he realized that she wasn't jealous. Kacie, and every other woman here, were not a threat to Ashley. Worrying about losing him had never even crossed her mind. She only cared about what it looked like to others.

Jealousy was an ugly color on her. Tonight, she wore a tone of self–righteousness. The way she thought she owned him disgusted Greg.

Nobody owned him.

Ashley resumed walking but stopped when he didn't follow. "What's wrong with you now?"

Nothing was wrong with him except for dating a bitch. His jaw tightened, and he glanced down the empty hallway. She had led him to a row of rooms on the ground floor.

One eyebrow lifted. Maybe she no longer 'had a headache' and it was payback time for the dress on her back.

He decided to follow her. The breakup would come later.

She put the pass card in the door and entered the room, where a group of people waited. With a polished, nothing–is–bothering–me smile, she stood in front of them and said, "David, Lily, Megan, you know Greg from our class."

The three stared back at him, and Greg guessed they didn't know who he was.

And if this were Ashley's way of making the night more magical to make up for the cost of the dress, David would have to leave.

Her head swiveled, and she stared at him. "You remember the old gang, right, Greg?"

Actually, no. If he remembered correctly, Lily was the snobbish bitch who never gave him the time of day; Megan never spoke to anyone unless she could gain something in return. And he was pretty sure David was the athletic hulk who had stolen his girlfriend senior year.

This wasn't his old gang. They were a part of Ashley's fan club.

And judging by how Ashley acted syrupy–sweet around them, he was apparently an object to be shown off.

His old gang was the basketball team, with Kacie his cheerleader urging him on to better things. Kacie had helped him fill out college applications, helped him select which school to go to, and had organized his going away party before his college freshman year. She had encouraged him to leave the nest and soar.

And now, ten years had passed, and Kacie was in love. In love with someone else. His chances—and he now needed to admit there had been many—were gone, leaving him with strangers in a hotel room.

It almost sounded like the start of a joke. "A man walks into a hotel room with three bitches and a bastard...."

Life had taken a turn for the worse, and he had been pulled away from Kacie for this? He knew nothing about

Kacie's fiancé, Braiden, except that he was the luckiest man alive.

"I'm glad you didn't have to file a missing person report on your new love interest." Lily studied Greg from head to toe. "He is tasty."

Greg didn't know what Ashley had told her fan club. He figured any fit, employed man who still had his hair ten years after graduation was a gold mine to some women. He certainly hadn't turned Lily's head back in the day.

That's when it occurred to him... Ashley saw him as eye candy. He looked better now than he ever did in high school, and she needed someone to show off to her gang.

How stupid could he be?

She was using him just as he was using her. He'd wanted to come to this reunion as a success. He was a divorcee, dating a demoness, and he just wanted to ditch the drama and find Kacie.

"I don't know what you have in mind, but I'm out of here." He opened the door and was about to leave when Ashley stopped him.

"We have a huge surprise for the reunion," she said.

A low whine came from the bathroom. Greg's head turned in that direction, but he didn't see anything.

"I don't know why I agreed to come to this event with you," he said.

Ashley glared at him, her fake smile changing into a scowl. "Come with me? You didn't even come to find me when you got here. I needed to drag you off the fucking dance floor."

She turned her head to smile politely at the other three

people in the room. Her hand gently massaged his. "But you're here now, sweetheart. So let's make the most of it."

Ashley rode her emotional roller coaster alone. He wasn't on it and had no plans to ride. "I'm done for the night. I'll see you at home."

As Ashley's fingernails dug into his hand, and her face twisted into a fiery evil visage, Megan said, "The mutt should be ready now."

"Stupid glue is still drying," David added.

Another whine came from the open bathroom door. A muffled bark followed. Greg stepped away from Ashley and walked to the noise. Hiding under the sink behind the trash can, he found a clump of light brown fur with a wet, black nose.

"There's a dog back here." He stepped closer.

"That damn mutt." Ashley let out a frustrated breath. "He's been nothing but trouble all night."

"He's in a bag or something." Greg reached out to the dog and said, "I won't hurt you, boy."

"It's his costume, silly, not a bag," Lily said. "He's our Royal Lion."

Greg knew the school's mascot. He just didn't understand why a scared dog hid behind the wastebasket. He moved his hand closer, and the animal whimpered and licked his hand.

The dog's soulful eyes besought him, and Greg finally saw him. He dropped to his knees and cradled the dog's face. "Skipper?"

He had left him at home and hadn't seen him since their morning hike since he had changed at the gym and came straight to the reunion. Now, the dog shook with uncontrollable fear. It reminded Greg of when he had first met Skipper. The dog had been hiding behind his crate, too afraid to come out and meet prospective owners at the pet fair.

Greg turned his head to stare at Ashley. "What the hell have you done to him?"

"I turned him into a Royal Lion. Doesn't he look great?"

Tugging at the mane, he realized the suit wouldn't come off. "He doesn't look great. He looks terrified."

"Dressing him was a bitch," David said. "A lion completes the reunion theme, though."

"Exactly." Ashley leaned over. "The dog is fine."

"He's a rescue. His last family abused him." Greg stood and faced off with her. "All the love and attention I've given him has only now allowed him to trust me, and now you do something this crazy. Are you insane?"

"Keep your voice down," Ashley said in a hushed tone so the other three wouldn't hear. "It's only fabric glue. She reached down and untied the leash. "He wouldn't keep the mane on."

"I don't blame him."

Skipper's reddened eyes and patches of fur missing from his face showed his pain. "He's trying to take the mane off," Greg said.

"No. Bad dog," Ashley snapped. "He's been fussy like this all day."

"You can't glue a costume to a dog." Greg finished untying the dog and inspected the rash all over Skipper's face. He tore off a small section of the mane. "I think he's allergic to the glue."

"You're going to ruin it." Ashley leaned over and smacked the dog on the nose, causing him to bare his teeth.

It was when she tried to reapply the loose fabric on his face that Skipper, with all his might, bolted and ran out the open hotel suite door.

11

Derrick approached the lone table in the back of the room. "We can leave if you want to." He placed another glass of wine in front of Kacie. "The only reason you had to stay is now spending time with his bitchy girlfriend."

She hadn't come to the reunion to spend time with Greg. At least, that wasn't the initial reason. Being a successful veterinarian and showing off her life seemed like such a petty reason. Still, she wanted to prove to everyone that she hadn't remained the wallflower, *Holly Hobby* of a girl that she was ten years ago.

And now, no one sat with her, no one talked to her, no one remembered her. The basketball players all knew her as Greg's best friend.

She even questioned if she knew herself. She had done such a great job of changing her appearance that she didn't recognize who she was anymore.

"I guess I expected more from this event than I should have."

"Reunion or not, Kacie, it's still high school." He pointed over to the dance floor. "Jocks." Then he pointed to a group of women near the bar. "Queen Bees." Then, gesturing to a smattering of women with their husbands, he added, "The wannabes who never became the Queen Bees."

Not that she remembered everyone, but Derrick had nailed it. The geeks and nerds sat at their own tables, and the potheads didn't even bother to show up.

Derrick shook his head and gave her a head nod accompanied by a sad look. "And the one man you wanted to impress isn't even here."

Her cheeks flushed. Was it that obvious? "I didn't want to impress Greg."

Derrick's eyebrow rose. "I was talking about Braiden."

"Braiden. Of course, I meant to say Braiden." Shame washed over her, thick and syrupy. She was nearly a married woman and had spent five years with Braiden. "A slip of the tongue," she said dismissively.

Derrick leaned in and touched her hand. "Tell me more about Greg and what he means to you."

It was the million–dollar question, one she didn't want to answer. "Greg is an old friend."

"An old friend who is…?"

He had been the crush of her life, back in the day. But he was more than that. So much more. "I could always talk to Greg. He was my go-to guy." She looked away and then added sadly, "The person I could fall apart in front of and know he'd always be there."

Derrick silently nodded, and then a spark twinkled in

his eye. "He's the one who stood by you during your mother's cancer, isn't he?"

It had been the lowest point of her life. Not knowing if her mother would live had emotionally wrecked her. Watching her lose her hair, sitting with her during chemo, and experiencing her down days. She had been strong in front of her mom, but Greg knew the truth. A river of tears, first sad and then happy ones when her mother survived, had been cried upon Greg's shoulders.

His strong and broad shoulders.

"He was my rock."

"You were in love with him throughout high school, and he only saw you as a friend."

Their friendship had started as forced playdates at the age of five so their mothers could spend time together. But that friendship had quickly grown right into the friendship zone—you could hang out together, but you weren't datable material. That's where it had remained for years. Where would it be today if college and careers hadn't interrupted their closeness?

"Now you have your chance. Tell him."

Derrick's words were soft and sympathetic, hinting at a gentle nudge. He was sweet to try, but he didn't understand. "Greg's with Ashley," she said.

"The hell he is. Good men don't settle down with that kind of woman."

In Kacie's experience, they did all the time. Beautiful men—truly rock–hard, handsome ones—always had a woman who was a perfect ten on their arms. At least one, if not two women glommed onto them. It left solid sixes, like her, to find men between five and eight on a scale of one to ten.

Braiden hit the scale as a nine, for the most part. As a plain–Jane, Kacie felt lucky to have landed him. He was handsome, wealthy, respectful… everything a woman would want.

Sorrowful tears threatened to escape. Braiden embodied everything a woman would want in a *roommate*. Gone were the passionate days. Gone were the days of intimacy when they stayed up late talking. Gone were her feelings of being a woman and pleasing a man since Braiden certainly wasn't interested in her body anymore.

Not that their passion had ever seemed romance–novel–worthy even at its hottest. Braiden scored a solid five in the bedroom, but not every woman could get a man whose fitting nickname should be *Tripod*.

"You'll see. Ashley is the kind of woman who…."

"What? Is beautiful and curvy?" she asked, cutting him off. She glanced down at her frame, knowing that Ashley resembled a rock star of womanhood while she belonged backstage with the roadies. Besides, Greg always dated the pretty girls, the ones who eventually broke his heart.

And Ashley would do that soon enough.

Not that it mattered. Kacie was engaged. She was with Braiden, and she was going to make things work. She held up her ring finger. "Besides, I'm with Braiden."

"And that man ain't here. You're having a miserable time at your reunion. That's not right."

Guilt bubbled up inside her for dragging Derrick to such a terrible event. "I guess I just wanted… I don't know." She waved at her hair and makeup. "I thought with the new style, I'd have a better time at this thing."

"You look incredible." He placed his arm around her. "Sweetheart, you are, by far, the prettiest woman in this place tonight. That haircut frames your face perfectly."

She took her phone from her handbag. "Then why hasn't Braiden said anything." She pulled up the text she had sent him and showed Derrick a picture of her with the new haircut. "He must hate it."

"And what if he does? Just proves the man has bad taste." Derrick shrugged. "Bad taste in hairstyles, not in quality women."

The nagging voice in the back of her mind returned and wouldn't shut up. *'Women.'* Had Braiden been cheating on her? He certainly hadn't been paying her any attention lately.

"What's with that look?"

The situation was embarrassing. She didn't want to admit that she wasn't happy, but Derrick was always there for her. She glanced around and ensured they weren't within earshot of anyone so no one could hear her shame. Even with the music playing, she whispered, "I think you're right. Braiden may be cheating on me."

Derrick let out a deep sigh. "Oh, honey."

It felt good to let it out, and Derrick's soft and supportive voice gave her the strength to continue. "He spends so much time at work, and even at home, he's not really there. I feel like his roommate half the time, not a lover."

"Do you have any proof that he's stepping out on you?"

It sounded stupid, but the first thing she thought of happened a few weeks ago. The minor incident had bothered her since. "A while ago, he made me some cocoa. Not a big deal, but he said he would make it how I liked it —with one and a half cocoa packages so it'd be extra chocolatey."

"And what's wrong with that?"

"I make my cocoa with exactly one packet. I put in less water." She shook her head, thinking that maybe she was crazy for such a minor thing, but there were many little things like that. "He also mentioned a restaurant for lunch and said we had eaten there before. But we'd never been to that place."

"A local restaurant?"

"Yes."

Derrick's face pinched, and he looked deep in thought. "Has Braiden ever shared his location with you on his phone?"

Location? She'd bared her soul to him, and he wanted to talk about cell phones? "I have no idea what you're talking about."

Derrick grabbed her phone and tapped the screen. "Really? Your passcode is your birthday?" he asked once he'd unlocked the device.

Not an ideal password, but memorable. "What are you doing?"

"Phones on the same plan have a hidden feature. If the phone is shared on the plan, you can see where it's been." He stared at the device and kept tapping and swiping.

"What does that mean?"

"It means you can trace his phone and find out where

73

he's been." He glanced up. "Don't you want to know if he's really on a business trip?"

She leaned in and held her breath. She hoped to find the man in California now, working, and in the office working hard for the past several weeks—just as he had said.

What if it had all been a lie?

The nerves of her spine prickled. She needed to know.

Derrick read the display and then glanced up from the phone. His eyes held the bad news. "He's in town."

"What?" Her heart pounded so fast it threatened to explode from her chest. How could he be in town? He was traveling on a prolonged business trip.

He turned the phone around so she could read it. "Says his phone is near the corner of El Salado Parkway and Hunter's Ridge Drive."

Shit.

Shit. Shit. Shit.

Kacie couldn't breathe. Braiden had lied to her. He'd repeatedly lied to her.

"That's near Terrytown, the expensive suburb." Derrick set the phone down. "Do you know who lives there?"

Fuck. Of course, she knew who lived there.

Braiden was having an affair with his assistant.

12

_____

"Five years!"

She had given Braiden five years, and this was how he treated her?

Hell no.

"He's not coming back for a few days. By then, I'll have the locks changed and all his shit sent to Goodwill." She paced the sidewalk in front of the Hilton, her high heels clacking with each heavy step. "I'll make him pay for this."

She held the phone and took screenshots. "I can see his whereabouts for the last thirty days. I'm going to document each time he went to her house and 'worked late,'" she said, her voice mocking the last part of the sentence as though air quotes surrounded her words.

"Kacie, he's not worth it."

Not worth it? Five frickin' years! "Derrick, I'm not going to let him get away with treating me like this."

"Do you love him?"

"Of course I do."

"Are you *in love* with him?"

What the hell kind of a distinction was that? They'd dated for years. "We're engaged." Her lungs couldn't fill with air, so she stopped pacing long enough to take deep breaths.

Derrick placed his hand on her back. "Luv, are you in love with Braiden? Is he the man you think of all day long? The man you want to spend the rest of your life with?"

Her thoughts felt cloudy, and she couldn't concentrate. Of course, she loved Braiden. They had lived together for the past three years, they had bought furniture together, they had made vows that one day would be spoken at church with rings exchanged. "That's what being engaged and getting married means."

"You're always in a more pleasant mood when he's not around."

She glared at Derrick. "That's not true."

"Kacie."

She glanced away. It wasn't true. Sure, Braiden didn't understand her devotion to animals. He didn't understand her passion for her vet clinic. He didn't understand her need to have a career and do something meaningful.

But her mood wasn't better when he was gone. She worried about him and wanted him back home. Naturally, she could spend more time at the clinic with him away. The extra time allowed her to look into things like adoption days and the idea of creating a no-kill shelter. Days like that were necessary. It gave her a sense of purpose.

She liked the extra time, but it wasn't about Braiden.

Hell, the man had only been to her vet clinic once in the last year. His presence there felt awkward, but she'd wanted to introduce him to her limited staff and show him around the place before he needed to get back to work.

The clinic was her haven, her special place.

Just like the house was when he went out of town.

She needed something more substantial to drink than wine.

It was true. Deep down, in the pit of her insecurities and self–doubt, a tiny girl screamed to get out. The little girl that was always last to be picked for a sports team, the child who always went to the school dances alone, the one who always settled yet wanted so much to be happy.

The little girl who one day wanted to be a successful career woman, a loving wife, and a dutiful mother.

It was the child inside of her who needed the truth. Needed to be loved.

That little–girl–turned–woman deserved to be happy.

And she was happier without Braiden.

"You are what I like to call a Little Sister. It's when a woman turns men into best friends, not boyfriends."

"I'm not a Little Sister."

"Sure you are. You were a Little Sister to Greg in high school, and you found me in college. You dish and share with the Big Brothers, but you don't date us."

She had many male friends, but there were other issues, too. "You're gay, Derrick."

"And gay men have a lot of Little Sisters because we're safe. Greg was your neighbor growing up, the son of your mother's best friend if I remember correctly."

"Yes."

"So, he was safe, too. Trust me. I've seen this before."
He gazed hard into her eyes. "Have you ever dated a man
you were friends with first?"

Her friendships with men—and there were many—
were close, and she had always been too scared to lose the
friendship. "Just because I've never dated a friend
doesn't—"

"And your relationships with men have fallen short."
His voice softened, and he added, "Your relationships are
missing the best part of you." He held up his hands. "On
one hand, you have the carefree, funny Kacie with whom
men love hanging out. On the other hand, is the sexy
woman." He clapped his hands together. "You need all of
you in a relationship. You separate yourself depending on
the man and the category you've placed them in."

Was it true? She and Braiden had met through a mutual
friend and had become intimate almost immediately. Her
other two physical relationships had been through a dating
app. Quick. Convenient. Bland.

Comfort and being herself around the men hadn't been
part of the equation. Beautiful dresses, fancy restaurants,
and pleasantries where she became who the men wanted
her to become the dating norm.

Her face flushed. None of her past loves had been
friends. They weren't her go–to guys, they weren't her
confidantes, they weren't even... A tightening in her gut
made her feel queasy. They weren't people she had
anything in common with. None had been soul mates.

She wanted a soul mate.

"Go after Greg. I saw the way he danced with you.
That man loves you."

13

"What do you want to do?" Derrick motioned back to the building. "We can go back in, we can call it a night, or I can take you out somewhere else."

Kacie stared at the hotel. The reunion didn't matter anymore.

Nothing mattered anymore.

Getting married. Having kids. Being happy. They were all ruined. Ruined because she wanted her bucket list of goals fulfilled so desperately that she'd become blind.

Her stomach twisted. Blind? She had suspected something was wrong with Braiden but had allowed herself to stay blissfully ignorant.

"Do you want to find Greg?" Derrick stared at her with a certain desperation that only a best friend wanting to make everything right could muster.

Greg dated Ashley. Kacie didn't need to see them together. The thought of them dancing, holding each other tightly, and kissing... no. She didn't need to see that.

"I'm going home."

Derrick wrapped his arms around her. "Call me if you want. I can rush over and destroy Braiden's stuff with you. We can even plot some revenge."

Kacie hugged him back, cherishing the warmth of his body and soul. "I know you're always there for me." She pulled away. "I'll be fine. I just need to think."

She wasn't sure what she would be thinking of. Braiden was history. That was a certainty. But she didn't know what to do. There were no overnight patients at her vet clinic, or she would go there.

Right now, she just wanted some ice cream and a bubble bath. She didn't want to think about anything.

She said goodbye to Derrick and walked the short distance to her car. Tomorrow was another day. She could think clearer tomorrow.

As she removed her keys from her purse, she heard a pained bark followed by shuffling leaves from the shadows. She turned her head toward the building and some bushes nearby.

She turned on her phone's flashlight and moved closer to the shrubbery, reminding herself to be careful. A wounded animal could be dangerous.

Lying on the ground and pawing at his face was a tan animal. She couldn't determine what it was, but she assumed it was a dog. "Come here, boy."

The tan animal whined and inched closer, causing what she assumed to be a doggy sweater to get caught on several twigs.

"Baby, what's wrong?" She held out her hand, and the dog sniffed her. He took another step closer, and she realized he wore a costume. He looked like a tiny lion.

She touched his snout, and the dog winced. Tiny globs of glue held down stuck whiskers and matted fur. The animal sat and held up his covered paw to shake her hand.

And that's when she recognized him. It was Skipper.

Greg's dog, Skipper.

The wind was knocked out of her. This was one of her patients. "Skipper, who did this to you?"

Tugging at the costume, she realized it wouldn't come off. "I need to get you to the clinic. Come on, boy."

From a distance, she heard, "Skipper!" She turned and saw Greg running toward her, followed by Ashley.

"Thank God you found him." Greg got on one knee and patted his dog. "I was so worried about him."

"Worried about him?" Kacie glared down at Greg. "He needs medical attention. He has glue in his eyes that needs to be washed out."

Ashley walked up, slightly out of breath. "The dog is fine. He needs to make a dramatic entrance to the reunion. I even have an app on my phone that makes the sound of a lion roaring."

Ashley was the last person Kacie wanted to see, especially with Greg. Everything Ashley had touched in high school ended up crap. She'd eventually bring out the stupidity and depravity in Greg if he were with her long enough. Too bad poor Skipper had to be around to see it.

Her jaw tightened, and she could barely look at Greg.

"The two of you are a pair." Kacie unclipped the shoulder strap of her purse and fashioned a leash out of it. "Skipper needs medical attention. Now," she said in a frosty, you're–such–a–dumbass tone.

"He needs to make an appearance at the reunion."

Ashley reached for the leash. "You can have him after that."

Kacie's glare bounced from one moron to the other, settling on Greg. She knelt and felt the dog's stomach. "What kind of glue did you use?"

"I didn't use…." He stared at Ashley. "Fabric glue. I think."

Kacie's fingers palpitated the dog's stomach. Thankfully, she didn't think the dog's gut was expanding with adhesive. "How much did you use?"

Greg glared at Ashley. "How much?"

"He wouldn't sit still. I think a full tube. Maybe a tube and a half."

"What size, Ashley?" Kacie asked.

Ashley's finger and thumb spread into about a two–inch stretch. "A few ounces."

Now checking Skipper's mouth, Kacie said, "I don't think he ate any. Just licked some. It's on his teeth and gums, but not in his gut."

"That's good news." Greg stroked Skipper's head. "He's a good boy."

"He's a *mistreated* boy." Kacie shook her head. "How could you treat Skipper like this?"

Greg's eyes widened. "I had no idea Ashley was going to do this."

Ashley now stood defiantly in front of Greg. "Sure you did. I told you about this, and you were fine with it."

"What? Never."

Daggers darted from Ashley's eyes. "Of course, you were. Last week, you said whatever I wanted to do was fine. Last night I told you that Lily and I had planned it all out."

"That's not what I… I didn't… You're crazy."

"You're both crazy." Kacie stepped away, tugging slightly on the leash and getting Skipper to follow. "I need to treat him."

"But we need him to be our Royal Lion mascot."

"Shut up, Ashley." Greg stood taller. "We're done. Pack up your shit from the apartment and get out. I can't be with someone who could treat Skipper like this."

14

Greg followed Kacie into the clinic and to one of the examination rooms. She turned on the light. "Put him on the table."

"I swear I didn't know anything about the costume or Ashley's plans." He got Skipper on the table and held him so he wouldn't fall, trying to soothe him as he did. "He gets nervous up here."

She opened the outer door and walked down the short corridor, only to return a moment later. "This is Acepromazine," she said, placing some into a syringe. "How much did he weigh last week?"

"Sixty pounds."

She injected the dog. "I need him sedated but awake."

"How can I help?"

"Here are scissors. Carefully cut what you can of the costume away. Be careful. Then, we'll need to bathe him."

Greg watched as she expertly rinsed Skipper's eyes and removed the glue from his gums and teeth. She moved from one area of concern to the next, with several rounds of "you're a good boy, Skipper," said to comfort him.

She was an angel. Thoughtful. Loving. Nurturing. She knew what to say and said it in a soft, reassuring tone. Skipper laid down and allowed her to work her magic, trusting her completely.

And all Greg could do was watch. This was precisely why his ex-wife had said he was a lousy father. He never took control, never took responsibility, and never knew what to do—except earn money.

Paying the bills was important, but being there for those who needed him was even more so.

When a child hurts, they want their parents. Not just a mother but also a father. All those business trips he had needed to take, all those late evenings he had needed to work, and all the boo-boos he had needed to kiss and make better but never did.

His children were still young enough that he could make a difference in their lives. Spend more time with them, play with them, and make every school function with them.

There would be time.

He'd make sure of it.

He removed pieces of fabric from Skipper's costume and tossed them to the floor, exposing more of Skipper's fur. With each bit of skin he saw, he petted Skipper and told him he was very brave and that Daddy was there to make it all better.

15

"Lift him and set him in this washstand." Kacie opened the door of the plastic bath and popped the drainage hole beneath so the water could drain out.

Gently, Greg placed Skipper in the tub, making sure to keep his head up. "It'll all be better soon."

Skipper's foot slipped, and Greg saw just how much fur Kacie needed to shave. It revealed Skipper's raw and tender skin. "I remember Ashley saying something about the king of beasts, but I swear, I didn't know what she was talking about." He glanced up at Kacie. "I'd never let her do this to him."

Kacie saw the worry in Greg's eyes as he cradled Skipper's head in his hands. The man cared about this dog. That was obvious.

So many people cared about animals. They just didn't take care of them. At least Skipper had seemed healthy and happy last week when Greg had brought him in. It was easy to believe that Ashley was solely responsible.

Kacie tried to focus on that and on the man she

remembered Greg to be. Kindness of heart wasn't something you grew out of. The man who'd stood by her all those years ago was still in there somewhere. Of course, Ashley's creepiness had dirtied him.

"Ashley would prattle on about so much," Greg said as he applied the special soap. "She usually talked about clothing and shoes. Following her conversations used to tax me too much. I'd usually just nod and say whatever. She probably did say something about this stupid costume. I just don't remember it."

"I believe you, Greg." In school, Ashley talked nonstop. The topic usually revolved around her, naturally. Kacie wasn't sure if anyone had ever listened to her.

No one had ever told her to shut up before. That's for sure.

Kacie carefully washed Skipper's face and ears. "I loved the expression on Ashley's face when you told her to shut up." Kacie couldn't suppress her huge smile. "I'll never forget it."

"She had it coming." Greg looked down at the half–asleep dog covered in soap bubbles. "Isn't that right, boy? That nasty, mean woman needed to go."

Kacie's hand massaged the soap around Skipper's back. Her fingers accidentally brushed against Greg's strong hand as he held Skipper in place.

Her eyes locked onto his. For the briefest moment, time stood still. Greg's suit coat was off, and his shirt sleeves were rolled up. He was a wet mess from bathing Skipper, yet he looked adorable.

Perhaps it was the love he felt for Skipper reflecting in his baby blues.

Perhaps it was his kindness for taking the dog in and seeing to his needs.

Perhaps it was more.

He washed Skipper's tail with one hand. Ashley had shaved the tail and left a tuft of fur at the end. It resembled a lion's tail. She hadn't been careful enough and had, unfortunately, left little nicks and cuts all the way down. Greg was gentle.

"Is Skipper going to be all right?"

"He'll survive." Her voice cut through the sound of the running water. "If Ashley prattled on so much, and you didn't listen to her, how could you be with such a monster?"

His eyelids lowered in what she thought was shame. "I don't even know anymore."

Ashley looked model beautiful. Kacie knew why men would put up with such a woman. What she didn't understand was how it could be worth the price. They'd still have to wake up with the she-devil the next morning.

She cut off the water. "We need to dry him and put some medicated cream on his rash and cuts. He should stay the night."

"I'll get him out of the tub."

Greg placed a towel over his dog and then picked him up. Skipper's half-shut eyes stared up at Greg full of trust and love.

And that was a test Kacie firmly believed in. If an animal trusted you, you were a good person. She placed a pad into a cage. "This warming bed will keep him cozy until he dries. I'll also start an IV if you can put this cone around his neck."

Greg glanced at the plastic cone. "He's going to hate this thing."

"We'll remove it once the rash dies down. Maybe in a day or two." She placed the IV and closed the door of the cage.

"I'll watch him until he falls asleep." Kacie wiped her hands on her vet smock and then removed it. Skipper's needs aside, she had enjoyed spending time with Greg. He had spent more time in her clinic than Braiden had over the last few years, and Greg took an interest in her career and trusted her with his dog.

It seemed foolish, but this evening felt special to her. She knew it couldn't last, though. She wanted him to stay but said, "You're free to leave if you want."

"I'm sorry about the reunion."

The reunion was the last thing on her mind. She was a vet first and had a patient. Nothing else mattered. "It's fine. I got to see the people I wanted to see."

"We never finished our dance." He glanced down at his soaked shirt. "I'm a little wet, but I'd love to have another turn around the dance floor with the prettiest girl at the reunion."

It was a bold move, but Greg wasn't ready to call it a night.

He pushed the Pandora app button on his phone and brought up music from when they were teenagers. "I hate the music of today. We had the best songs back then."

He walked to the light switch and dimmed the lights before reaching out his hand. "May I have this dance?"

The shy smile she gave him was all Kacie. It was the same one she had given him when she won the science fair their junior year, when she had told him she'd be interning for the local vet her senior year, and when he hugged her goodbye and left for college after graduation.

His heart pounded and sounded as though it were stuck in his ears. Hopefully, she wouldn't notice his sweaty palms. She'd probably think the slickness was only due to Skipper's bath water and not because he felt terrified.

He was asking another man's fiancée to share a dance. A private dance. It had been easy to dance with her at the reunion in a room full of witnesses, but this was different.

It felt more intimate.

She closed the distance between them, and he held her tight in an embrace. The ballad the app had played was their prom theme—slow and seductive. It was only by chance that the song had been selected, but it was perfect for the moment.

He hadn't danced with her at the prom. It had never occurred to him to do so, even after the dance had been moved to the football field after the flooding rain. Now, their private "vet clinic" dance became all-consuming.

Her soft hand held his, and lightning shot through him. This was Kacie. His Kacie. The girl he used to make fun of as a child, the one he would tell all his secrets to, and the one he could always be himself around.

She let out a small sigh, and her breath brushed against his neck.

Do it, he thought. *Just lean down and kiss her.*

Her warm body swayed, pressed flush against his as

they danced. The chorus repeated once more, and the song was nearly halfway done.

Don't be stupid, he thought. *Kiss her.*

She glanced up at him, her blue eyes piercing the dimly lit room and melting his heart. He only smiled back.

Stupid.

He had kissed so many women in his life. Why would kissing Kacie be so difficult? He had the perfect opportunity, and he'd just let it slip by.

He didn't know when she'd be tying the knot. But time ticked away. He didn't know her fiancé, didn't care. She wasn't married yet, and there was an opportunity, however slight, that he could make Kacie see him as more than just an old friend.

He didn't kiss her, but he allowed his hands to slip lower and curve around her thin waist. A slight moan escaped her, and he took it as a good sign. Another few inches and he would cradle her firm backside.

Being already half-hard just having her this close was torture enough. He didn't need to be thinking of her bottom, or her long legs, or the fact that her chest now pressed firmly against his own.

Right now, he just wanted a kiss.

Wanted to taste her full lips. Devour her mouth and kiss her so hard that she'd forget all the past men in her life. Forget about her fiancé.

He licked his lips. The chorus repeated, and he knew the song would soon be over.

He felt like a kid playing hide–and–seek with the person who was it already up to nineteen out of twenty in counting, and he still hadn't found a place to hide.

Why did his heart have to pound so hard?

"Greg?" Her soft eyes caught his, and then her gaze lowered to his lips.

He stopped swaying to the music. This was it. This was their moment.

He leaned down and kissed her. Tenderly at first, but then matching the pressure of her desire. Her hands entwined in his hair, and he gripped her firmly, allowing the passion to sizzle between them.

16

K acie had been busy over the last two weeks. She checked her list once more. She had already found an apartment, opened a new bank account, and moved her few personal items out of the house. There was one more thing left to do.

She stared at the last item remaining on the list. Break up with Braiden and return his house key.

It would have been easier to do if he had been home over the last two weeks, but no. His so-called 'business trip' was followed by, what she assumed, was a legitimate business catastrophe that had him suddenly leave town.

And, according to the app on her phone, he actually did leave town this time.

She paced the hallway at the vet clinic. His plane would be landing now, and she had a good hour before seeing him. Her hand clenched in a fist. She wanted to teach the lying cheat a lesson, but right now, she just wanted the ordeal to be over.

"I can lock up," Derrick said as he walked past her

carrying a sack of diet dog food. "I'll finish unloading this prescription food and close up. Everyone else has already left."

She followed him to the back room. "I should leave, but I'm not in a hurry tonight."

Derrick put down the food, stacking it on a pile of others. "Are you thinking of taking Braiden back?"

Her job dropped. There was no way in hell that was going to happen. She gave him her best 'are–you–kidding–me' expressions.

His hands went up in surrender. "I'm just making sure."

She sat at the tiny table in the back of the room and glanced at the day's mail. "It would be nice to torture Braiden first, but I'm tired of games." She sighed deeply and said, "I'm ready to get this over with so I can…."

"Start dating Greg?" Derrick's eyebrows waggled. "I know you have had some dinners out, but you're not calling him your boyfriend just yet." He took a seat next to her. "Is something wrong with Greg?"

"No." Her cheeks flushed. Derrick knew everything about her; there were no secrets, so she said, "We've gone out a few times, but until I officially break it off with Braiden… nothing can *really* happen yet."

"You're too good of a woman, Kacie Preston." He shook his head. "Most women I know would have already had that man a dozen different ways—and in Braiden's bedroom, no less."

She rubbed her head and then stared upward, letting her shoulders droop. "I've been so tempted. I can't even tell you."

It was killing her. Greg had been a perfect gentleman, which fueled the flames even more. His understanding, gentleness, and downright rugged, handsome good–looks. If that man smiled one more time and said, 'you're worth the wait,' she'd strip down and take him where he stood.

She was already feeling the heat of her body just thinking about him, so she thumbed through the mail to get her mind on something else.

Bills, bills, more bills. A letter in a brown envelope caught her attention. It was from her high school friend Steve. Her lease on the vet clinic was nearly up, and she had contacted him about possible locations.

An email from earlier in the day was from Grady with some advertisement estimates once she moved her clinic to a different location. She grinned, thinking about how much Greg had supported her and the clinic. Even his friend Ned would help out with social media ads.

Things were moving so fast. And Greg was so sweet to talk to Grady on her behalf. He really had her best interest at heart.

"What else is bothering you?" Derrick took the letter from her hands and set it down. "Something else is wrong."

There had been something eating away at her, and she didn't like it. It was more than just relocating the clinic and breaking up with Braiden—even though those two items are a considerable part of her life now.

No. What bothered her was how much she felt she needed Greg in her life. She never thought of herself as a woman who defined herself by the man she was with, but all she could think about was how lucky she was that he had come back to town. "Am I turning Greg into a rebound man?"

Derrick let out a boisterous laugh. "Kacie, you are one woman who has always been cautious. Cautious to a fault, honey." He held her hands. "Most women I know have no clue what they want or how to get it. They rush into everything—especially romances."

"You don't even date women, Derrick."

"Uh-huh. That's no accident." He cleared his throat and leaned in. "You are not someone who makes life changes easily. But you are someone who has always followed her heart."

"And look where it's gotten me."

"People get cheated on. That's not on you. That's on Braiden."

She took a deep breath and let it out slowly. "Can I trust my heart? Or am I looking for an easy way out of one relationship by jumping into another one?"

"Kacie, your heart has never let you down." He glanced around the tiny room, his arms fanning out. "You followed it when you chose what career to have. You followed it when your mother was sick all those years ago. And you're following it now to dump that lame–ass Braiden."

Those decisions had been the right ones. But was Greg different?

"What is your heart telling you about Greg?"

The loaded question lay heavy on her chest, but honestly, she knew she wanted to be with him. "I want to date Greg. See where it takes us."

"Then follow your heart, honey."

EPILOGUE

"Greg, the puppies need more water out front." Kacie walked past him with a fluffy, white cat in her arms and a big smile on her face. "Mr. Whiskers just got his forever–home."

That was the tenth adoption today, and it was only noon.

"We can refresh the water bowls, Dad," Greg's son said, grabbing one of the buckets of fresh water. His sister grabbed a second one, and the two went to the front of the store.

"Thanks for having the kids help out. This place is packed." Kacie walked to the register and gave the cat to Derrick. "This one is ready to go," she said, smiling at the young couple waiting to adopt him. "Remember to give them a coupon book for the hospital's grand opening."

She glanced around the clinic, now turned into a non–kill animal shelter and full hospital. Location made all the difference. Her old friend Steve had been right about that.

He'd managed a great deal on a corner lot for them where an old fabric store used to be. The building was huge, and the advertising Grady and Ned offered proved invaluable. The clinic, now called *Bisset Animal Clinic*, named with their joint surname, was doing well.

"Honey, we got some more donations." Greg carried a box of puppies to her. "Six weeks old. I'm not sure what breed they are, but the man that dropped them off said he didn't want them."

Two puppies poked their heads out of the box and yipped in her direction. "People need to spay and neuter their animals if they don't want a litter of little angels." She patted one of the Yorkie pups, and the diamond in her wedding ring caught a ray of light from the overhead lamps, reminding her of how happy she had been the last year. "I'll give them a quick examination. Maybe we can get them out in the playpens for adoption this afternoon."

She reached for the box, but Greg stopped her. "Let me carry them to the back for you, sweetheart. You need to take it easy. You're seven months pregnant, after all."

She rubbed her belly and was thankful that she had built the life she wanted and hadn't settled. Greg's kids were spending the summer with them and would be there for the baby's birth. They had an entire household—the two kids, Skipper, and a baby on the way. She and Greg were blessed. Plus, they had adopted three puppies over the past year. Their house was definitely a home.

The End

I hope you enjoyed reading my short story, More Than Puppy Love. Please leave a review on the retailer site where you purchased your copy of the book. You can find a link to all retailers at http://www.reginamorris.com/more-than-puppy-love-info

ABOUT THE AUTHOR

Dear Readers,

Please visit my website (http://www.reginamorris.com) for more information about my other novels and short stories. Feel free to contact me through my website, my social media sites (see my website for the list), or email at mailto:reginaannmorris@gmail.com?subject=Email%20from%20fan .

I like to play games and have fun with my newsletters. Please sign up at http://newsletter.reginamorris.com.

I mostly write romances and the heat level differs from mild to hot. My short stories involving the Historic Preservation Agency and time travel are mild. My vampire and billionaire romance novels are hot. These hot stories have an age warning of 18+ on them.

My husband and I live in the heart of Texas in our two-story, red-brick dream house. Our home has plenty of air conditioning, carpet, and pillows to comfort our two spoiled Sheltie puppies, who never leave my side. Our adult children have left the nest but are still in Texas and only a short drive away.

The opinions I express in my novels are my own. My stories are my intellectual property. Copyright (c) 2013–2023, Regina Morris

Sincerely,
Regina Morris

ACKNOWLEDGMENTS

Special thanks to my husband and our children for their love and support; to my sister for believing in me and encouraging me to follow my dreams; to my critique partners, Jean and Pennie, for being with me every step of the way; to my editor Chelle (Literally Addicted to Detail); and my proofreader team. I also want to thank my beta readers and street team of supporters. This book would not be possible without the support I have had from all of you.

OTHER BOOKS BY REGINA MORRIS

Time Travel books

Historic Preservation Agency

Time Historian

Rich Indulgence Billionaire Series

Bachelor Heart

Bachelor Soul

Bachelor Dad

Bachelor Doctor

Short Stories

Taking Chances

Christmas Joy

More Than Puppy Love

www.ingramcontent.com/pod-product-compliance
Lightning Source LLC
Chambersburg PA
CBHW030552130626
46552CB00006B/2509